"Do you think we've lost them?" Anna whispered.

"I hope so."

"You don't sound confident."

"If they're local, they'll know that most of the mines have two entrances. They may have gotten maps from the historical society that gave them ideas of where they could..."

"Hide a body?" she asked, completing his thought.

"I figured it might be best not to say that."

"Why? It's not like I don't know what they were planning. Either kill me and make it look like an accident or kill me and make certain my body was never found."

"If you disappear, the star witness ceases to be a problem."

"You really do know who I am," she said, her stride easily matching his. She ran a few miles every day on the ranch. He knew her routine the same way he knew the routines of his other employees. Ranches, like farms, could be dangerous, and he considered it his responsibility to make certain the people who worked for him stayed safe.

Anna wasn't just any employee.

She was his newest freelance job.

Aside from her faith and her family, there's not much **Shirlee McCoy** enjoys more than a good book! When she's not hanging out with the people she loves most, she can be found plotting her next Love Inspired Suspense story or trekking through the wilderness, training with a local search-and-rescue team. Shirlee loves to hear from readers. If you have time, drop her a line at shirlee@shirleemccoy.com.

Books by Shirlee McCoy

Love Inspired Suspense

Hidden Witness

FBI: Special Crimes Unit

Night Stalker
Gone
Dangerous Sanctuary
Lone Witness
Falsely Accused

Mission: Rescue

Protective Instincts
Her Christmas Guardian
Exit Strategy
Deadly Christmas Secrets
Mystery Child
The Christmas Target
Mistaken Identity
Christmas on the Run

Visit the Author Profile page at Harlequin.com for more titles.

HIDDEN WITNESS

SHIRLEE McCOY

LOVE INSPIRED SUSPENSE

INSPIRATIONAL ROMANCE

LOVE INSPIRED® SUSPENSE
INSPIRATIONAL ROMANCE

Recycling programs
for this product may
not exist in your area.

ISBN-13: 978-1-335-57459-6

Hidden Witness

Love Inspired
22 Adelaide St. West, 40th Floor
Toronto, Ontario M5H 4E3, Canada
www.Harlequin.com

Printed in U.S.A.

Thou wilt keep him in perfect peace, whose mind
is stayed on thee: because he trusteth in thee.
—Isaiah 26:3

To my one and only search-and-rescue flanker buddy, the sole person in my world who never gets tired of hearing me ponder aloud the meaning of life. Thank you. You know why. If you don't, check the handbook. Page 325. Article 1. Subcategory B. It's there.

ONE

Annalise Rivers waited in darkness, crouched deep in a thicket of brambles, cold seeping through the thin fabric of her running gear. High above, the full moon gleamed between branches of mountain ash and sour gum. She shifted her weight, trying to ease the pain in her cramped thighs and calves. A thorn scraped her neck, but she didn't dare shove it away. They were hunting her, and one wrong move could give her away.

A branch broke and a man cursed, the sounds carrying on the still winter air. He was close, the thicket a buffer between them—a protective shield that she hoped would keep her hidden. Light danced across the ground a few yards away, the beam bright enough to illuminate the thicket floor. She didn't sink back into the foliage, afraid of the noise she might make. If the light found her, she'd run. If it didn't, she'd wait. Eventually, someone at Sweet Valley Dude Ranch would realize she was missing. A search party would be sent out, and her pursuers would flee.

She hoped.

Anything was possible. She'd been a criminal defense lawyer long enough to know that. She'd also been one long enough to know that she should have stayed at the ranch instead of going on an evening run outside the safety of its gates. She hadn't been placed in Witness Protection because the threat against her was minimal. Archie Moreno wanted her dead. He was desperate to make it happen. As an eyewitness to the murder of Archie's former second-in-command and the only witness who had seen the shooter, Annalise had the potential to help put one of the country's most notorious mobsters away forever. Of the three survivors of a courthouse shooting that had taken two lives, Annalise was the only one whose testimony could be key to taking down the Moreno crime family.

A light bounced off the top of a bush to her left. She tried to make herself smaller, to sink into the frozen ground and be covered by dead leaves and debris. She thought she heard the staticky sound of an open radio line. There. Gone. The line closed as the hunters moved in on their prey.

A second light bounced across thick vines and thorny branches a few yards to her right. Did they know where she was? Was that possible? She'd been attacked three miles from the ranch, on a trail she had been running. She had fought off her assailant and escaped into dense foliage. She had no idea what direction she had run. She had no clue where the ranch was. Thousands of acres of wilderness surrounded her. Yet, somehow, she couldn't seem to escape her pursuers. It made no sense, but she didn't have time to think about it. Both lights went out, plunging the thicket into darkness. She heard the unmistakable sound of a gun safety being released. She didn't think, she moved, dropping to her belly and army crawling through the tangle of briar bushes. The first gunshot hit the ground inches away. The second blew through the branches above her head.

She scrambled backward, shoving through the thicket, not caring how much noise she made. They knew she was there. If she didn't escape, she would die. A third bullet struck the ground in front of her, splintering dead branches. She froze. Afraid of making the wrong move. Of crawling into the path of the next bullet. She didn't want to die. Not out here in the middle of nowhere. Not before she had a chance to live all the dreams she had put on hold for her career.

A fourth shot split the night, and she cringed, expecting to feel the impact. Instead, she heard a high-pitched cry of pain and the unmistakable sound of retreat. Branches breaking. Twigs snapping. Feet pounding on nearly-frozen earth. Then, silence.

She had no idea what had happened, and she wasn't going to wait to find out. She crawled out of the thicket, staying low and moving fast. The moon was bright, her night vision clear. She scanned the area. No flashlights. No dark shadows moving through the trees. She was alone.

Or seemed to be.

A creek burbled nearby. She could hear water swirling over rocks and pebbles. A stream or creek would lead to civilization. At least, that's how it always seemed to work in movies. She'd find the stream and follow it until she reached a house or business. It wasn't a great plan. There were probably a million holes in it, but it was the only one she had.

She headed toward the sound, picking her way down a steep ravine. Her feet slipped as she reached the bottom. She grabbed a sapling to keep from falling.

She needed to be more careful. If she fell and was injured, she would never make it out alive. She made it to the creek bed and followed the flow of water as it bubbled across smooth stones. She was heading downstream. She knew that. Hopefully, downstream would eventually lead to a house, a road or a business.

She had no idea how far she was from safety. Sweet Valley Dude Ranch was a two-thousand-acre working cattle operation located ten miles west of Briarwood, Texas. There were thousands of acres of hill country and wilderness surrounding it. If she didn't make it out on her own, she doubted a search party would be able to find her. She was a tiny speck of humanity in a vast expanse of woodland. Easily lost. Not easily found.

A branch snapped at the top of the ravine, the sound sending chills down her spine. Had they found her again? It didn't seem possible or probable. They'd left while she was in the thicket. She hadn't seen their lights or them when she had exited it. And, yet, she couldn't shake the feeling that she wasn't alone.

She whirled toward the sound.

She had no weapons.

No armor that could protect her from bullets, but she would face whatever was coming head-on.

And, she would fight.

She expected a frontal attack.

She was grabbed from behind, a steel-like arm wrapping around her torso. A hand pressed over her mouth. Everything happened so quickly, she didn't have time to turn, to scream, to run. Her arms were trapped at her sides. She kicked, trying to connect with a knee or shin, threw herself backward desperate to unbalance her attacker. His grip tightened.

"Stop. They're still out here, and I have a limited supply of ammo. We need to keep quiet, okay?" a man whispered in her ear, the voice vaguely familiar.

She nodded.

"You're not going to scream if I release you? You're not going to run?"

She shook her head.

His grip eased, his arms dropping away. She spun to face him. Saw the cowboy hat first. The five-o'clock shadow. Broad shoulders. Eyes that looked straight into hers. A familiar face to go with the familiar voice.

Very familiar.

"Mac?" she whispered.

MacArthur Davis owned Sweet Valley Dude Ranch. He had hired her to assist his cook who prepared meals for dude ranch guests and for the ranch hands. He didn't know her real identity. Just the fictitious one assigned to her by the US Marshals. He had no idea that she was witness to a murder. Or that a very dangerous man wanted her dead.

"You need to get out of here," she whispered.

"We need to get out of here," he corrected.

"Mac, you don't understand—"

"I understand perfectly. Now, how about we both be quiet before we draw attention to our location. I'm not in the mood to die tonight. I'll explain things later. The guys who were shooting at you headed back toward the trail. We need to move in the opposite direction," he murmured.

"You saw them?"

"Not well enough to provide a description, and I'm not sure how many there are. At least three. That's as much as I know." He took her arm. His grip was firm, his fingers warm through the silky underlayer beneath her running vest.

She had been working for Mac for six months, but she didn't know him well. The ranch kept him busy. Cooking kept her occupied. When it didn't, she found other things to do. Most of them involved staying away from people who might ask questions she couldn't answer. Living under her assumed name with her assumed background had begun the afternoon she had arrived at the ranch with a newspaper help-wanted ad for a cook clutched in her sweaty palm. It had been July. Putridly hot, and she had been driving the old pickup truck the US Marshals had procured for her. She had been hoping she'd be turned away and that the Justice Department would have to hide her in another location. After all, she had known nothing about Texas and very little about cooking.

It hadn't worked out that way.

She couldn't say she was upset about it.

Not anymore. She had learned a lot during her stay at Sweet Valley.

"This way." Mac gave her arm a gentle tug.

Her mind had been wandering.

She had been wandering.

Away from the stressful situation and the fear.

She needed to stay focused and alert. She didn't want to be taken by surprise again. Earlier, she had been running on the trail, thinking about Boston when a man had said her name: Annalise Rivers. A name she hadn't heard in six months. She shouldn't have responded. If she hadn't been thinking about the past, maybe she wouldn't have. She had turned, caught a quick glimpse of a ski mask and dull blue eyes. She'd been knocked to the ground, pulled off the trail as she fought and clawed to free herself. Somehow, she had managed to grab a stick and jab it into her attacker's throat. Not enough to stop him but enough to loosen his grip. Annalise had broken free and run.

She had escaped, been found again, escaped.

Next time, she might not get away.

She and Mac stayed close to the creek. Steep hills rose to both sides of it. She didn't want to think about how easy it would be get trapped in the creek bed, unable to scale the muddy banks that jutted like walls on either side.

"What if—" she began.

"Shhhh," he hissed.

She had never been one to follow blindly. She preferred to take the leadership role, but right now, she could see no way out of the trouble she was in except to do exactly what Mac said.

Be quite and keep moving.

One step after another.

Away from the men who were following and toward some unknown destination that she could only pray would offer them shelter and safety.

In the years since MacArthur Davis had first agreed to allow his ranch to be used as a secret safe house for the US Marshals, he had never come this close to losing a witness. Then again, most of them had been short-term placements. His ranch had been a halfway house of sorts. A place for endangered witnesses to stay while they waited to enter the witness protection program. Mac's old buddy, US Marshal Daniel Avery, had recruited him years ago, offering good money in exchange for the use of the ranch. Men and women. Young and old. They had come with new identities and stayed as guests. Annalise had been different. Mac had known that going into the assignment. She was the sole witness to a murder, and her testimony could link the killer to one of Boston's most notorious crime bosses. Daniel wanted her to stay on the ranch until the trial. Under an assumed name and assumed background, she had been working as a cook, staying in one of the cabins reserved for ranch hands. He had been keeping an eye on her. Just as he had all the other witnesses, but instead of the two months Daniel had estimated, the placement had dragged on for six. Good money. Enough to pay off the second mortgage on the family ranch. But it wouldn't be worth it if he died. Or if she did.

He eyed the muddy walls that rose up on

either side of the creek bed. He knew this area well. He'd spent his childhood summers exploring the wilderness around the ranch. If he could get them out of the creek bed and onto higher ground, he might be able to get cell phone reception and call for help. If not, their best hope was to make it to town without being spotted by the men who had been shooting at Anna.

He hadn't been close enough to count the number of assailants, but he had been plenty close enough to put a bullet through the gun arm of one of them. That had been enough to chase off the group, but maybe not enough to keep them away. He scanned the gray-black forest, searching for light, for moving shadows, for any hint that they were being hunted.

The wilderness was eerily quiet. No deer picking their way through the late winter foliage. No raccoons out scavenging for food. The moon hung low over the trees. Full and bright enough to enhance visibility, it was both a blessing and a curse in a survival situation like this.

He stopped at a large tree that had fallen across the creek, tested its strength and then shimmied up and out. Anna was right behind him, her quiet breathing and the gentle rustle of fabric catching on branches the only sounds she made.

He offered her a hand as she reached the top, pulling her up and out easily. The hair on his nape stood on end. His body hummed with adrenaline. He knew these woods. He knew the peaceful solitude and quiet that sunset brought to them.

This wasn't it. He didn't dare pull out his phone, afraid the screen light would give away their location. The tree-cover was thicker farther from the creek. He led Anna there, jogging up hill and deeper into the forest. Decades ago, the area had been mined extensively. Now, it was pockmarked with abandoned tunnels and man-made caves. He had explored many of them. If he could reach the closest, they would at least have cover from gunfire while he planned the next step of their escape.

"I don't like this," Anna murmured, her voice breaking through the unnatural quiet.

He didn't either, but he wasn't going to tell her that. No sense adding to her worry or doing anything that might call attention to their location. They were heading across a ridge that protruded over the river. He could hear the rush of water far below. Large boulders stood sentinel over a nearly sheer three-hundred-foot drop. He dragged Annalise around the closest one, desperate to get her out of the line of fire.

"Stay here." He whispered so close to her ear, he could feel loose strands of her hair tickling his lips.

"Where are you going?" She grabbed his arm, her eyes wide, her pale skin nearly glowing in the moonlight. She wore dark leggings and running shoes, but her long-sleeved T-shirt was white, her running vest bright blue.

"I want to see if we're being followed."

"I'd rather keep moving. Together," she replied, her hand still on his arm.

"I'm not going to abandon you here, Anna. I'll be back for you."

"I'm not worried about me. I'm worried about you. There are men with guns out there," she hissed.

"I'm armed." He tried to reassure her, but she shook her head.

"You're one against many. Those aren't good odds."

"Stay here," he repeated. He didn't have time to argue with her or to explain that he had spent years in the military working special ops.

He eased around the boulder, staying close to its granite face. Moonlight glittered on mineral-rich earth and painted the treetops white-gold. It was a beautiful night. The kind that had drawn him back to Texas and to the ranch after he had been medically discharged from the Navy. He had longed for the slow-pace of small town life, the busyness of the cattle business, the feel of being home. He'd had no idea his grandfather had mortgaged the property to help pay for his grandmother's cancer treatments. He hadn't known how far in arears the payments were. He had just known that he wanted to be where life made sense.

He scanned the area below the ridge, spotted a quick flash of light that could have been a dimmed flashlight beam or a cell phone. Either way, he and Anna weren't alone. They were being followed. He wasn't sure how they were being tracked so easily. The wilderness was vast. The possibilities for their escape endless, but Anna's assailants seemed to be heading straight toward their location.

He rounded the boulder and grabbed her hand, dragging her toward the cliff that overlooked the river.

"If you're planning to drag me over the

edge of the cliff, I'd rather take my chances here," she said.

"There's a way down."

"One that doesn't require wings or a parachute?" she asked, glancing over her shoulder. She didn't ask what he had seen. Maybe she didn't want to know.

"Now isn't the time for jokes," he muttered.

"That wasn't a joke," she responded.

"Stay close," he warned as he stepped between two boulders and found the path that wound down to the river.

"I wouldn't dream of doing anything else," she murmured, her voice shaking, her fear palpable.

He couldn't blame her. To their left, the earth fell away, pebbles clattering over the edge of the narrow path that had probably been carved into the cliff hundreds of years ago. It had been shored up and used by miners in the early twentieth century—the treacherous path leading to the entrance of a mining tunnel that had been blasted into the hillside.

Light cut through the grayish night, dancing on spindly trees that speared out from the sheered hillside a dozen yards away. They had minutes before Anna's assailants reached the top of the hill. Maybe less. He picked up his speed, knowing they were like fish in a barrel—easily picked off by gunmen shooting from the above.

Annalise stumbled. Just a little. Just enough to make his pulse jump and his breath catch.

"Careful."

"Trust me. I'm trying to be. I'm also trying to hurry. Those lights are a little too close for comfort."

"We're almost there."

"Where? The bottom?" She stumbled again.

"Don't look down, okay? Focus on the path. There's a mining tunnel a little farther down. We'll duck in there."

"And do what? Wait for them to track us

there? We'll be trapped, and I'm not interested in having that happen."

"We won't be trapped. There's another exit. I wouldn't go in it otherwise." He picked his way down a narrow man-made path that opened onto a wide ledge. The cave was a dark hole in a pale sea of exposed granite. They reached it as an avalanche of pebbles and dirt rained down on their heads.

"Get inside," he urged, as he nudged Annalise through the four-foot opening. More dirt splattered onto the granite as he followed her into inky darkness. Seconds later, gunfire split the silence. Bullets pinged off the rock at the mouth of the cave and the earth trembled. Old beams that had been used to shore up the roof of the cave groaned and the entire hill seemed to shift.

He had anticipated gunfire.

He hadn't anticipated this.

A cave-in could easily do the assassins' jobs for them.

Mac couldn't let that happen.

"Move!" he shouted, grabbing Annalise's arm and yanking her deeper into the cave as a small cloud of dust and particles filled the opening. He kept moving, his hand tight around Anna's arm as they raced through the darkness. An avalanche of shale, old wood and dirt followed, the dust from the collapsing cave, filling his lungs and coating his skin.

He couldn't hear anything over the roar of falling debris, but he could feel Anna coughing, her body shaking with the force of it. He hadn't brought her to the cave to die, but if they didn't keep moving, that might be the outcome.

He sprinted forward, dragging her with him, praying that they could make it to safety before the entire mine collapsed.

TWO

Annalise's lungs filled with dust. Her throat felt clogged with it. She coughed and gagged but could hear nothing above the sound of the mine's thunderous collapse. She didn't want to die. Especially not in a mine, buried by tons of dirt, in a place where no one would ever find her.

And, Mac…

He had a ranch to run, people relying on him, a business and employees who all depended on him being around. What would happen if he didn't return? How would the people she had met, that she had come to care about during her time on the ranch be affected if he died because he had been trying to help her?

She couldn't think about that. She had

to focus on keeping up with his breakneck pace. They ran through the darkness as if it were broad daylight and they were in the middle of a clear field.

Dirt rained on her head as wooden beams splintered and cracked. She tried to scream. Maybe she did scream, but the sound was lost in the chaos. She tripped, would have fallen if Mac hadn't yanked her upright.

He was moving fast, but he didn't seem panicked.

He didn't seem scared.

She was both.

She needed to calm down.

Think.

Plan.

Execute the plan.

Survive.

It was simple.

How many times had she done the same when she was growing up? All the years of making certain that her mother was okay, that medicine had been taken on time, that bills had been paid, had taught her the importance of logic and reason, of focus and positivity. Her mother, Doreen, had been eighteen when Annalise was born. Kicked out of the house by parents who didn't understand her mental illness and who had no desire to help her, she had done what she needed to survive on the streets. She might have stayed there, trying to care for a baby and hustle for food, if an elderly woman at the church that Doreen attended hadn't taken pity on her and offered her a room in exchange for housekeeping and cooking. Annalise had a few memories of Lucy Richards—a white-haired woman with a cane who had always had a smile and a hug for her. With Lucy's support, Doreen had managed to get her GED, a good job and a nice apartment. Most of the time Doreen had been fine. When she wasn't, Annalise took care of things. She cooked meals, cleaned the house, paid the bills. Her father had been out of the picture. His family wanted nothing to do with her. Doreen's family refused to acknowledge her. After Lucy passed away, it had been Annalise and Doreen against a world that had often seemed unkind.

But, God was good.

That had been Doreen's answer to everything.

God is good.

Annalise knew He was, but sometimes it was hard to see the light through the darkness. Sometimes it was difficult to see His plan through the pain.

She tripped again, her head glancing off the wall.

Mac shouted something.

All she heard was the whooshing of dirt filling the tunnel behind them.

They rounded a sharp corner, her shoulder slamming into granite as Mac tried to steer her in the direction he wanted to go. The walls were closer, the air clearer, the rumble of the collapse fading as they continued to run. She had no idea how far they went, but she was panting when Mac stopped. She stumbled to a halt beside him, eyes straining to see into the darkness.

"Hold on a second," Mac said. Fabric rustled. Light filled the tunnel, so bright she could barely see.

She blinked, trying to force her eyes to adjust.

"That's better," Mac muttered, the beam of the light tracking across the dirt floor and up one of the walls. "You okay?"

"I think so," she responded, coughing through the words. "Unless we can't find the second entrance you were talking about."

"We'll find it."

"And, if it's blocked?"

"We'll move onto plan B."

"Which is?"

"I'll figure that out when we get to it," he replied, sweeping the beam of a small flashlight along old wood that had been used to shore up the dirt walls.

"We could have used that light when we were running," she pointed out.

"I was more worried about getting you out of a bad situation than I was about getting a light out of my coat pocket," he replied. "Come on. The sooner we get out of here, the sooner we can call for help."

"You know the way?" she asked.

"Yes. I spent summers exploring this mine when I was a kid."

"Your parents allowed that?" she asked, appalled and intrigued by the idea. She could almost picture Mac as a kid, exploring the tunnels. Perhaps making up adventure stories and acting them out with friends. She had been too busy keeping things together at home to play those kinds of games, but it was what she had always imagined her children doing.

When she had imagined she would have children.

Before all her plans had fallen apart.

"My parents didn't know. I spent a few weeks every summer at the ranch. My grandparents ran it, and I ran wild when I wasn't helping out," he responded, moving forward again, his pace brisk, his stride long. He had a no-nonsense approach to running Sweet Valley Dude Ranch. She had been paying attention, collecting information on the way he interacted with wealthy guests and employees. Not because she had a case to build against or for him, but because she had been curious and bored. Cooking for guest and ranch hands took time, but it didn't take a lot of mental energy. She was used to having information for cases filling her head, trial dates filling her datebook. She wasn't used to being still and quiet.

"That sounds like a great way to grow up," she murmured.

"It was. You grew up in the city?" He met her eyes. He had lost his cowboy hat, and he looked different without it. Tougher. Harder. More like a soldier than a ranch owner.

"I did. In Boston."

"You don't have much of an accent."

"I studied law..." Her voice trailed off

as she realized what she was about to reveal. She was supposed to be from Dallas. A transplant from the big city looking for work in a small town. Not a defense attorney working for the FBI who had just happened to be at the wrong place at the wrong time.

"You studied law where?" he prodded, taking the information in stride. As if every cook he hired had once studied law.

"In Tennessee. I probably lost the accent while I was there." She answered truthfully. There was no sense keeping up the pretense. Not when Moreno's hit men had already found her.

"Vanderbilt?"

"Yes."

'One of my Navy buddies attended law school there."

"Small world," she murmured, surprised that he wasn't asking more questions about her law degree, her real reason for being in Texas, the lies she'd told on her application.

"I know who you are, Anna, and I know

why you're in Texas," he said as if she had spoken her thoughts out loud.

"I don't know what you mean." There might not be much reason to keep up the pretense, but she had spent six months pretending to be someone she wasn't. She didn't feel comfortable admitting the truth. Even now. While they were running from the men who Moreno had hired to kill her.

"Sure, you do. I was contracted by the US Marshals to offer my ranch as a temporary safehouse for people in the witness protection program."

She stopped short. "Are you saying you've known who I am from day one?"

"Yes." He'd stopped too, turning to face her, the flashlight pointing to the ground and illuminating the dirt floor of the mineshaft. "Daniel Avery and I go way back. We were in the Navy together."

"Daniel Avery?" she repeated. Not because she didn't know who Avery was, but because she was surprised Mac did. Her location and her identity were supposed to be top secret. She had been warned not to contact anyone from her old life and not to tell anyone in Texas who she really was.

"The US Marshal who brought you into the program?"

"I know who he is. I'm just surprised you do. I was told no one in Texas would know my real identity."

"As far as I'm aware, no one else was supposed to. Obviously, someone does."

"Who?" she asked, knowing he didn't have an answer.

"We'll figure it out after we get out of here." He started walking again, the beam of his light illuminating the darkness and chasing some of Annalise's fear away.

"How long has it been since you've actually used the other exit?" she asked, still worried that they would find their only other means of escape blocked.

"A while."

"So, it could be blocked?"

"It could be."

"Great."

"What?"

"I was hoping you'd tell me there was no way it was blocked. That we were going to get out of here without any problem. If you told me there was an entire squadron of police officers waiting to escort us back to the ranch, that would be a bonus."

"No police, but we shouldn't have any trouble getting out of the mine."

"And back to the ranch?"

"Let's tackle one problem at a time," he responded.

"So, you're admitting this is a problem?"

"Are you wearing your attorney hat? I feel like I'm being interrogated."

"Sorry. I like to have a clear plan of action."

"We have one. Get out. Get to safety. Find out who leaked your location. Get you back to Boston for the trial."

"There are a whole lot of things that could go wrong at any point in that plan," she muttered.

"Let's focus on what we're doing now instead of what could go wrong later, okay?"

He was right.

They needed to focus on what was. Not what might be.

Here and now was what mattered.

Finding a way out.

Getting back to Boston and putting Moreno and his hit man away would come after that.

She followed Mac through the narrowing shaft, the beam of his light bright enough to guide the way around turns and through even narrower passageways. The weight of the earth above and beside her seemed to press in, stealing her oxygen and making breathing difficult. She inhaled deeply, the scent of damp earth filling her nose. She had never been claustrophobic, but she suddenly felt trapped, her heart beating frantically as she imagined wandering the underground tunnels forever.

"Don't think about it," she muttered.

"You okay?" Mac called over his shoulder.

"Fine," she lied.

"You sure?"

"Absolutely."

"Good, because if you were going to panic, now would not be the time to do it. We're almost at the mouth of the mine shaft, and I don't want noise to carrying to the guys who are after you."

"I don't believe in panicking."

"Good to know, because there's going to be some climbing involved in getting out of here."

"Climbing?"

"The opening is about twenty feet up. There's a ladder. Or there used to be."

She didn't bother asking what would happen if the ladder no longer existed. If it had broken, fallen, was damaged beyond repair.

"I know how to climb a ladder."

"Great, because we're here."

He stopped. She had a quick glimpse of a small cavern before he turned off the light. For a moment, the world was completely dark, cold air wafting in through a hole Annalise couldn't see. As her eyes adjusted, she could make out an opening high above. Moonlight filtered in, casting shadows along the floor. A ladder was attached to the wall, stretching up to the opening, its spindly rungs narrow. She touched it, her hands sliding over rough cold metal.

"It's rusted," she said.

"It's been here a long time," he responded, giving it a gentle shake. "I climbed it a few times when I was a kid. It was sturdy."

"It's a few years older now," she replied, her gaze on the ladder.

"And, I'm a few pounds heavier. It was built to last." He shook it again. "But it might be best if you climb it first."

"And, if it breaks, you won't follow?" she joked.

"If it breaks, I'll catch you," he replied. "If it doesn't, you'll be out of here before we take a chance on my weight." He pulled a cell phone from his pocket and handed it to her. "As soon as you're out, see if you're able to call 911. Stay low. Keep your voice down. We don't want to call attention to ourselves."

"All right." She tucked the phone into the pocket of her running vest and put her foot on the lowest rung. The ladder groaned as she took the first step up.

"Slow and steady," Mac urged.

She nodded, swallowing a hard knot of fear.

"Wait," he said before she could take the next step. "Your shirt is too light. You'll be easily visible. Put this on over it."

He shrugged out of his coat and dropped it around her shoulders. She shoved her arms into the sleeves and rolled them up, too focused on the impending climb to argue about whether she should take his coat.

She eyed the mine opening, cold air bathing her hot cheeks. She didn't want to do this, but Mac was right. If he climbed the ladder and it broke, they would both be stuck in the mine. If she made it out, she could call for help.

"Anna? You need to get up there before your friends figure out that there are two entrances to the mine," Mac urged, his tone just sharp enough to grab her attention.

She nodded acknowledgment and started climbing, the rickety ladder shaking, her heart hammering. She wanted to pray for safety and help, but her mind was numb, her thoughts scattered. All she could do was hold onto the cold metal, pull herself up one slow steady step after another and trust that God knew exactly what she needed and exactly how to help.

The last thing Mac wanted to do was let Anna precede him out of the mine, but he couldn't risk breaking the ladder before one of them escaped. There was no cell phone reception in the mine, and until they were out in the open, they had no way of calling for help.

"Be careful," he cautioned as she reached the halfway point. He could see her silhouetted against the circle of sky, his coat falling to her knees, her hands pale on the dark ladder rungs. Once she crawled out of the hole, she would be out of sight and too far away for him to help if she needed it.

"Remember. Stay low when you get out," he called, risking being heard to offer one more word of caution.

She didn't respond. He assumed she understood how easy it would be for her voice to carry through the opening and out into the night air. Sending her ahead was the riskiest thing he had done in a while. He could feel adrenaline coursing through him and the razor-edged focus that always came with it.

Watch her climb out and follow.

Quickly and carefully.

Don't spend time thinking about what could go wrong.

Work toward the goal and achieve it.

The thoughts rushed one after another

through his mind as he tracked Anna's upward progress. Five more feet. Two. She reached the lip of the opening and scurried over.

He started up at a sprinter's pace, the ladder shaking as his booted feet met old metal. The craftsmen had built the ladder to last, but it had been hanging for decades, the rungs giving just enough to make his heart pump harder.

He was a halfway up when a rung gave. His foot slipped, and the ladder swayed. He swayed, too, his hands gripping slick metal, his heart thumping rapidly.

"Are you okay?" Anna peered into the opening, her head and upper torso blocking the light.

"Fine," he responded, scrambling up the rest of the way.

She grabbed his hand as it curved over the lip of the opening. Then his wrist, her fingers digging into his skin as she tried to tug him out.

He didn't need the help, but he didn't tell her that.

The less they said, the less likely it was that their escape would be discovered.

"I tried to call 911, but there's still no—"

He pressed his palm over her lips. No pressure. Just a warning. Then dropped it away, motioning for her to follow. They'd exited the mine at the base of the hill. He scanned the area, searching for and finding lights moving along the ridge above. Two hundred meters away, they appeared and disappeared through the winter-bare trees. The ridge and hill were between Mac and the ranch. The main road that led to town was in the opposite direction, farther away but a safer option.

If the gunmen didn't realize that he and Anna had escaped.

He took her hand, leading her away from the mine shaft and deeper into the woods. The moon was high and full, the forest easy to navigate without a light. This time of year, ground cover was sparse, the deciduous trees barren, their gnarled branches providing little cover. He stayed close to the trees, moving as quickly as he could. Winter silence made every snapping twig or breaking branch echo loudly through the cold air. In the distance, a man shouted, his words muted and inaudible.

If the gunmen were locals, they would know about the mines that pockmarked the hills. They would be looking for a second entrance point, and if they found it, they might be able to track Mac and Anna.

"Do you think we've lost them?" Anna whispered, the words puffing white in the frigid air.

"I hope so."

"Hope?"

"It's better than the alternative."

"Which is?"

"Hopelessness. We've got a head start. How about we focus on keeping it?"

"I'm focused. I'd just like to know the plan," she said, her stride easily matching his. If she was scared, she wasn't showing it. His coat slapped against her knees, the cuffs falling over her hands. She had a layer of grime on her face and a bruise on her cheek. She had nearly been shot, nearly been buried alive and was being hunted by men who wanted her dead, but she was moving confidently, heading into the woods as if she didn't have a worry in the world.

That intrigued him.

She intrigued him.

From the moment she had arrived on the ranch, he had been drawn to her positive attitude and exceptional work ethic. She had been uprooted from her life in Boston. She'd gone from working as an attorney for the FBI to working as a cook on a dude ranch. She'd handled it with aplomb and grace.

"The plan is we head to town."

"Isn't the ranch closer?"

"There are men with guns between us and it. Closer isn't the better option."

"So, we're walking to Briarwood."

It wasn't a question, but he nodded. "It's the closest town. We can head straight to the sheriff's office and see if we can get some protection out at the ranch. I'll call Daniel from there."

"He won't be happy. Someone leaked my location to Moreno. Only a few people are privy to the information." She shoved her hands into his coat pockets and frowned. "You better take this back. It's cold."

He stopped her before she could shrug out of the coat. "Keep it on. I'm wearing dark clothes. You're not."

"I wasn't thinking about trying to stay invisible out here when I left the ranch."

"You shouldn't have left the ranch," he pointed out. No judgment. Just a fact.

"I know. It's just..."

"What?"

"Six months is a lot longer than I expected to be here. It's a long time to be away from home. I've been restless. Ready to get back to Boston."

"Your family will be there when you return."

"I don't have any. But my job keeps me busy. I like the people I work with. I like the mental challenge. No offense to chefs and cooks, but peeling potatoes and cutting up onions gives me way too much time to think."

"About?"

"All the things I should have done before I got myself into this mess."

"You didn't get yourself into anything. From what I understand, you happened to be at the wrong place at the wrong time."

"It was the right time, if you're the prosecuting attorney in the case. A clear-minded witness who is absolutely certain of what she has seen is a rarity in a murder investigation."

"But, it's not the murderer that Daniel was worried about when he sent you here," he said, glancing over his shoulder. The lights were still there, moving through the woods behind them. Not coming in close, but not getting farther away.

It seemed improbable that the gunmen knew the direction Mac and Anna were traveling. It would make more sense to head back to the ranch. Less than two miles away, it was the easier path to safety.

"No. He was worried about Archie Moreno. Godfather of a mob family in Boston," she said.

"I'm familiar with him."

"Prosecutors have been able to link him to the shooting I witnessed. They think, with enough pressure, the gunman will confirm that Moreno paid for the hit. If Moreno can silence me, the prosecution won't have a strong enough case and their bargaining power will be gone." She glanced back. "They're still coming."

"I know."

"They can't possibly know we got out of the mine. Can they?"

"I don't know, but how about we keep quiet and keep moving?" He cupped her elbow and picked up the pace. He didn't bother telling Anna that he knew everything about the shooting she had witnessed and everything there was to know about Moreno. Daniel had filled him in before Anna's arrival. Forewarned was forearmed. Mac had been on high alert, his security systems and security staff working overtime. For six months everything had gone well. And, then, Anna had broken the rules, left the ranch alone and ended up on the wrong side of several guns.

Someone had been watching the ranch, waiting for an opportunity to strike. Anna had unintentionally given it to him.

Mac was going to make certain that didn't happen again. From now until the trial, he was going to be glued to her side.

"See the hill in front of us?" he asked.

"It would be a little hard to miss," she replied wryly.

"The road to town is on the other side of it." He glanced back, his pulse jumping when he caught a glimmer of light through the trees. It was closer, their pursuer obviously moving in.

"What's wrong?" she whispered.

"Maybe nothing."

"How about you give me worst case scenario?"

"They're closing in because they have someone in front of us who can cut us off from the road."

"How is that possible? They were nowhere around when we left the mine. We're not using a flashlight. They shouldn't be able to see us." She glanced back, tripped over a fallen tree and nearly tumbled over.

"I don't know. We still have distance between us, so let's just keep focused."

"Right," she muttered.

He picked up the pace, leading her straight up the side of the hill. If he had the higher ground, he could hold off gunmen for a while. He would rather not have to do that. He wanted to get to safety, get backup and figure out who had leaked Anna's location to Moreno. Until he did, she wouldn't be safe.

He was being paid to hide her on the ranch, but his obligation went deeper than that. He had to keep her safe. He had to get her to trail. Mac was completely committed to making certain both those things happened.

No matter what it took.

THREE

Mac was a straight shooter. She had asked for the worst-case scenario. He had provided it. And now, she wished she hadn't asked, because the hill was even steeper than it had looked, the terrain rock-strewn and covered with fallen trees and brambles. Making progress felt like slogging through chest-deep mud—painfully slow and difficult. She told herself not to look back, to keep her eyes and her mind focused on what lay head.

But, of course, she didn't listen.

Just like she hadn't listened to her smarter, wiser self when she decided to go for a run outside the perimeter of the ranch. She had gone against the little voice in her head that had told her she was still in danger and that she shouldn't let her guard down and wander away from the safety of lights and people.

And *this* had happened.

Life didn't work out well when a person got distracted from the goal. She knew that. She should have applied that maxim. Even here, at the edge of civilized and modern life, where trees were more abundant than people and giant wild hogs roamed the underbrush, it was better to have a plan and stick to it, to reach unwaveringly toward the final prize. No looking back and wondering or worrying that a wrong choice had been made.

She glanced back anyway, just a quick look to see if there were lights below. She slipped on shale and leaves, her feet going out from under her so quickly she had no time to respond. She grabbed for a tree or bush—anything to keep from tumbling down the hillside.

Mac grabbed the back of her collar, halting her progress. He didn't release her as she scrambled to her feet, panting hard, heart bucking like the wild horses she'd seen being tamed in the corral in the west pasture of the ranch.

"Focus," he said quietly. No heat or panic in his voice, no hint that they might run out of time if she didn't get her act together and start climbing again.

"Right. Sorry."

"No apology necessary. Just keep moving." He let her go and headed up again. He moved like she imagined a mountain lion would—sure-footed and confident.

She was more like a newborn giraffe, tripping and slipping, tumbling and getting up again. She grabbed a sapling tree, tested it for strength and hauled herself another few steps.

"Are you sure this isn't a mountain?" she whispered, her lungs burning with effort. All the marathon running sessions in the world could not have prepared her for this kind of hustle.

"Does it matter? We have to climb it

one way or another." He responded in the matter-of-fact way he used with the city-dwellers and suburban families who paid good money to vacation at Sweet Valley Dude Ranch. Most of them were as clueless about ranch life as Annalise had been when she'd arrived. He never treated them like they were stupid or inept, but he seemed to have perfected the fine art of breaking information into manageable snippets that even the most clueless guest could understand and apply.

"Right," she murmured, refusing to look back again, but also determined to not look any farther ahead than was necessary. She didn't want to know how much farther they had. She didn't want to think about how much her lungs burned and her legs hurt. She sure didn't want to imagine what would happen if she gave in to exhaustion and sat for a while.

They climbed for what seemed like another hour but was probably only minutes. Then, like the first streaks of dawn after the darkest night, the ground leveled out and they were done.

There was no celebration, of course.

No victory dance under the full moon.

A group of men had been hired to kill her, and Annalise could no longer pretend that maybe the US Marshals had overreacted. That maybe the Justice Department was worried about nothing. She had to face the facts that she had been avoiding since she had agreed to leave Boston. She could die. Just like Thomas Ryland had.

She could still hear the bullets, if she let herself. She could see the look of shock on Ryland's face as the first bullet struck him in the chest. She had been feet away, heading down the stairs outside the courthouse. Feeling great about winning another case. It had been way past time for her to be home, the late spring evening ripe with the scent of fresh-cut grass and exhaust. She had no one to go home to, and she had hung out at the courthouse way too long, chatting with other attorneys, with judges and with the bailiffs she had come to know so well during her time as an FBI defense attorney. The place had emptied out, and she had been alone, packing up her briefcase and heading out for another quiet night in her apartment.

She had seen Thomas Ryland as she exited the elevator. She'd had no idea who he was. The criminal case against his boss had made the news, but she had been nose-deep in her own case, working to defend a special agent who had been accused of excessive use of force. She'd had no idea who Ryland was. She'd only noticed him because he was in ankle shackles and cuffs, flanked by uniformed officers. Edmund Richards was a few feet ahead, looking through a file folder. Richards had been the state prosecuting attorney. She'd been up against him enough to know how tough he was.

They had walked out of the courthouse just ahead of her. She'd been lollygagging, not ready for the long weekend that was ahead. She'd had no plans, and she had been telling herself she didn't want any. She liked being alone. She liked her independence. She liked having no one to answer to but herself.

She had been giving herself that pep talk as she stepped outside, heard the squeal of brakes as a car sped around the corner. She had looked and seen the vehicle, the bright streetlights glinting off its black hood. The passenger window had been open. She'd seen a face she had recognized, and then the first shot rang out.

She shuddered, not wanting to remember the fear on Ryland's face. The shock. Not wanting to think about the blood spurting from his chest. The frantic shouts of the police as they pulled firearms. Richards falling, the folder spilling papers across the courthouse steps.

"It's okay," Mac said, suddenly standing in front of her, his hand on her cheek, warm palm against cold skin.

"I know."

"Then why are you crying?"

She hadn't realized she was. She wiped the tears away quickly. Crying had never done her any good. It certainly wasn't going to help her now.

"It's cold. My eyes are watering," she lied.

"Okay." He studied her for a moment, his hand still resting on her cheek.

It felt oddly intimate and comforting.

Surprised, she stepped back.

His hand dropped away, and he began walking again, as briskly as before. She matched his pace, following him across the hilltop and down the gentle slope of its west side. Unlike the climb up, the way down was easy—moonlight brightening the forest, the tree growth sparser. They wound their way downhill, then onto flat ground split by a narrow creek. She didn't ask if they were close to the road. She didn't want to know if they weren't. Right now, she was focusing on taking the next step.

A light flashed in the trees, straight ahead and moving quickly.

"Was that a car?" Annalise whispered.

"Yes."

"We made it." Her legs went weak with relief.

"Let's not celebrate yet."

"Celebrate? I'm just happy to not be walking through the woods anymore."

"We're going to stay in the woods. That'll be safer than walking on the side of the road."

"How many cars drive down this road this time of night? I don't think we need to worry about being hit."

"I'm worried about being seen by the guys we left in the woods. They didn't walk into the area. They had transportation."

"What's the likelihood that they'll be back at their vehicle and on that road in time to see us walking to town?"

"Considering that they've managed to track us from the mine, I'd say pretty good."

"Track us?" She swung around, nearly falling in her haste.

"Just keep moving," he replied, snagging the sleeve of the coat he'd lent her and tugging her forward.

She wanted to run, and she would have, but he held her back.

"They're far enough away that we should be okay. Let's stay calm and careful," he chided.

Should?

She hoped he meant *would*.

She didn't ask. Up ahead, the trees opened into a wide expanse of grass. Moonlight glinted off a guardrail that separated a drainage ditch from the road.

"We're going to cross the street and walk in the woods on the other side. Ready?" Mac asked.

She'd barely had time to nod when he grabbed her hand and took off. They sprinted across the clearing, down into the drainage ditch and up the other side.

He didn't release her as he stepped over the guardrail and darted across the street.

The wind had picked up, dead leaves skittering across the pavement. There were no headlights, no engine sounds, no tires swishing over the road.

And then there were.

High beams cut through the darkness as a car sped around a curve in the road and headed straight for them.

"Get down!" Mac shouted, tackling her to the ground and covering her with his body. Tires squealed. Gunfire split the air. And she prayed that no one would be killed.

They were being tracked.

Not just by men on foot who knew how to follow Mac and Anna's footprints. There had to be a tracking device on Anna. Mac couldn't think of any other way that they could have been found so easily.

He waited until the gunfire stopped, raised up just enough to fire his Glock toward the road. A warning shot more than anything, to let them know he was armed, and that he wasn't afraid to shoot.

"Take off your pack," he whispered as he edged up and got a view of the vehicle—an older model Ford Explorer, the license plate hidden by dirt.

"What? Why?" Anna responded, already shrugging out of his coat.

"Anything in there you need? Wallet? Money? Keys?"

"No. Just water and a couple energy bars."

"What else are you wearing that could hide a tracking device?" The SUV was rolling back, the engine idling. The driver was waiting for someone. Probably the men who'd been in the woods.

"Nothing."

"No belt?"

"No."

"Phone?"

"No."

"Shoes?" He shifted his attention to her feet.

"Of course I'm wearing shoes," she murmured, a hint of fear in her voice.

"You have a pedometer on one."

"Right. Can we get out of here instead of discussing my clothing options?"

"They're tracking us. I need to know how so we can stop them."

"Okay. Aside from the pedometer, I don't carry anything when I run."

"Your watch?"

"It's been on my wrist forever. I don't take it off."

"Okay. Let's go. If they're still able to track us, we'll get rid of the pedometer."

"How about we do it now?" She had untied the shoe and was pulling the pedometer off the lace. She tossed it onto the ground, and he grabbed it, flipping it over and looking at the underside. A small tracking chip was adhered to it.

"This explains a lot," he muttered, his mind racing for an explanation. He was certain that Anna had been asked to give up everything from her old life. He had to assume the shoe pedometer was new. Something purchased after she had left Boston.

If that was the case, how had the tracking device been placed on it?

Someone from the ranch.

Someone Mac trusted.

Someone who had betrayed that trust.

He scowled, tucking the tracking device in his pocket.

He could hear feet pounding across the grassy field across the street. Their pursuers were closing in.

"Let's go," he said, grabbing Anna's hand as he belly-crawled through the ditch. South. Away from town and toward the ranch. There were trees close to the road there, and as soon as he thought they had enough cover, he yanked Anna up and into the woods, sprinting hard.

They were moving fast, dodging trees and ducking through thickets of brambles.

Behind them, branches cracked and men cursed, the dense foliage making going difficult.

A river cut through the valley. He headed there, knowing the water was high and fast enough to keep the tracking device moving. Anna was panting hard, keeping up. Barely. If they didn't lose their tails soon, they might not.

When they reached the river, he pulled the tracking device from his pocket and tossed it in. Eventually, the water would destroy it. That was fine. All he needed was a little extra time.

He veered right, heading north again, following the winding path of the river upstream. There were a few cabins in this area. Tucked into the woods and looking out over the river, they belonged to die-hard fishermen and hunters who spent weeks out in the woods during the spring, summer and fall. They were empty now, their dark facades visible as he and Anna raced past.

"Have we lost them?" she panted, her breath wheezing out, her body trembling. He wanted to stop and let her rest, but they needed to get to get to town. He had planned to call the ranch and ask for help, but he had no idea who had planted the tracking device. It could have been a guest, but he suspected it was someone a lot closer to home.

"I hope so." He slowed, his hand wrapped around Anna's, his mind buzzing with adrenaline. He had been in situations that were just as dangerous and faced off with more determined enemies. He had never done it with a civilian by his side.

"Have you ever thought of lying for the sake of making someone feel better?" she muttered, the words panting out.

"No. Now, how about we keep quiet until we're safe?"

She didn't respond.

He took that as a good sign.

The sounds of pursuit had faded. He hoped that the tracking device signal had lasted just long enough to throw their pursuers off and send them running in the wrong direction. Once he made it to town and contacted someone in the sheriff's office, he could make plans. He didn't know where he and Anna were going, he didn't know how long they were going to be there, but they weren't spending the night in Briarwood or the ranch. And they weren't contacting the Justice Department with their whereabouts. Not until Mac made certain there wasn't a leak in the system.

Or proved that there was.

He couldn't think of any other way Anna's location had become known. Someone who had the information had been paid well to give it away. Mac needed to find out who if he was going to keep Anna safe.

FOUR

Briarwood looked like the stereotypical small town—shops standing shoulder to shoulder on a two-lane main street. Old houses on pretty lots. Fences. Sidewalks. A library. School. Diner. Bakery. A few small businesses that catered to the town's eclectic interests. Yarn. Crafts. A feed store. A small doctor's office stood at one end of town. At the other end, a used car lot, a bar called the Watering Hole and a run-down trailer park.

Once a week Annalise and the ranch's head cook went to town for supplies. While they were there, they went to the local grocery store, visited the library for books, ate at the diner once in a blue moon. During the past six months, Annalise had

come to appreciate the easy pace of Briarwood. She'd come to know the people. She
had begun attending church every Sunday
morning, riding in with the van of people
who came from the ranch.

She had never been to the sheriff's office.

She hadn't thought she would have a reason to.

She had been told that the local sheriff would be aware of who she was and
why she was in town, but she had never
verified it. There had been no need. She
had been so far away from everything she
had known, so far away from that horrible
night, the gunfire, the blood, that she had
sometimes been able to forget that she was
the target of a man who had money and
power at his disposal.

She shouldn't have forgotten.

She should have been on her guard every
minute of every day.

And she would be.

Once they reached the sheriff's office.
Once she was safe.

She told herself that was going to happen.

She had been through tough times before. She had made it through with determination, hard work and faith. This was no different.

"We're almost there," Mac said, his breath puffing out in a white cloud. The temperature had dropped, the wind whipping the grass that edged the two-lane road leading to town. The trees were sparse, the way lit by intermittent streetlights. In the distance, more lights gleamed from porches and windows, the soft glow beckoning them forward.

"You've been saying that for forty-five minutes," she responded.

"Your teeth have been chattering for the same amount of time. I was trying to keep you moving."

"You didn't need to worry. I'm not stopping until we get to the sheriff's office. I want these guys caught. Once they're behind bars, they might decide that giving up the name of the person who hired them is better than spending twenty years in jail."

"And you think that's going to be Moreno?" he asked, glancing over his shoulder, his head cocked to the side as if he had heard something.

"It'll be one of his thugs. But thugs talk, and a connection with Moreno will only make the state's case stronger."

"I like your optimism," he said.

"It's not optimism. I defended a few cases like Moreno's before I started working for..." She stopped herself before she could give more information. Mac knew some things. He didn't know it all. For his safety, and for hers, that was for the best. Once they reached the sheriff's department, he could go back to the ranch and his life. She would go to whatever safe location the Justice Department decided on.

Just until the trial.

Which could be next month or next year.

She hadn't cared about the timeline when she'd been talking to the new prosecuting attorney for the state. Richards had died on the courthouse steps, taken out by the man he had been trying to put away.

"For the FBI," Mac completed her thought, then grabbed her hand and pulled her up beside him. "Once we walk out of the woods, we're in the open. There are houses, cars and business that we could use as cover, but I don't want to risk more lives."

"I don't either."

"The old church is just through the trees. Do you remember it?"

"Brick. With a bell tower and cemetery." She had to pass it each time she came to town.

"There's a shed at the back of the property. I want you to wait there while I get the sheriff."

"You're kidding, right?"

"I don't joke about life-and-death matters."

"I'm not hiding in a shed, Mac."

"You'd rather walk through town and

risk being shot or having someone else shot? This is a small town. There isn't much space between houses. One stray bullet and a kid could die. Or an elderly person—"

"Any loss of life would be tragic. You don't have to keep trying to convince me," she muttered. His reasoning was sound, but she didn't love the idea of hiding in a shed while he went for help. Having him risk his life to save hers wasn't something she was comfortable with.

"What if you hide in the shed, and I go for the sheriff?" she whispered as they stepped out of the forest and into a field of tall grass and shrubs.

"They're after you. Not me."

"I'm pretty certain they're after both of us now."

"I don't think they know who I am. Even if they do, shooting me is going to accomplish nothing. They may follow me to try to find you, but they aren't going to take me out."

"I like your optimism." She repeated his words and was surprised when he met her eyes and smiled.

"It's not optimism. It's weighing options and finding the least risky one. If you stay in the shed and stay quiet, we should both be safe."

"Why would I leave?"

"Why does any person do anything that might harm them? Because you think you have a better plan? Because you're worried that I'm not coming back? Because you hear people moving through the yard and think they're onto you?"

She could imagine being influenced by any one of those things. She was prone to going her own way and making her own decisions. She knew how to take advice at work. She had been mentored by some great defense attorneys. But in her private life, there had been no one to tell her what to do or give her advice since Gabe had left.

"I'll stay in the shed because I couldn't

live with myself if anyone else was hurt because I didn't."

"Was someone hurt because of you?" he asked as they moved through the field and walked up a gentle hill. The church was sitting at the top of the rise, long grass hissing quietly in the breeze.

"No," she said, but in her heart, she didn't believe it.

She had heard the car tires squeal. She had seen the car speeding around the corner. She still wondered if she could have saved Richards. If she had shouted a warning, tackled him, screamed, would that have made a difference in the outcome?

"Okay," he said.

"Okay what?"

"If you don't want to talk about it, I understand."

"Talk about what?"

"Whatever it is you think you could have done to save the men who died." They had reached the crumbling asphalt that had once been the church parking lot. Sprigs of grass jutted out from the broken pavement. Life springing from unlikely places.

"I didn't take you for a mind reader, Mac."

"I know what it feels like to watch someone die. I know how hard it is to not replay it, add to it, put more time in for reaction and heroic deeds." He answered matter-of-factly, his tone even and emotionless.

If they had been anywhere else, if he had been anyone else, she would have asked him if he was okay. If the past still haunted him. If the lives he hadn't been able to save made him want to live with more passion, with more purpose, with deeper conviction.

But they were running from men who wanted her dead. He wasn't the kind of guy who ever showed strong emotions. She doubted he wanted to share his story.

And they were heading past the cemetery, across the parking lot and into what had once been a playground for church kids. Now the swings hung listlessly, the slide covered with debris. Beyond it, an overgrown field gave testimony to ball games and church picnics. She couldn't see a shed, but Mac seemed to know where he was heading. Through the field, back to the edge of what had once been cleared ground. Now it was dotted with sapling trees and briars.

Annalise didn't see the shed until they were right in front of it. The aluminum siding was dented and rusty, the painted double doors peeling. There was a padlock hanging from a chain between the metal door handles.

"It's locked," she pointed out, as if Mac wasn't capable of seeing that for himself.

"Yes. It is," he agreed, taking a multi-purpose tool from his pocket and bending over the lock.

Seconds later, the chain fell away and the door creaked open. Something scurried in the dark interior, the sound sending cold fingers of fear up Annalise's spine.

"Was that a rat?" she murmured.

"Probably not."

"That is not reassuring."

"You have men with guns chasing you, Anna. Would you rather face them?"

"Maybe," she replied.

"No," he corrected. "If there's an animal in there, it's not going to bother you."

"There you are with that optimism again," she muttered.

"I'm stating a fact. Go inside. I'll have to lock you in. There's a window. My grandparents attended this church when I was a kid, and I used to help my grandfather mow the grass. If I don't come back—"

"How about we stick to optimism?"

"If I don't come back, you'll be able to climb out the window. Just be careful. If you see lights, find a way to hide. If they look in the window and see you…"

"Don't worry. I'll make sure they don't."

"Good. You're sure you're okay with this plan?"

"What if I'm not?" She leaned into the shed, trying to see through the darkness.

"Then we'll come up with a new plan."

"Really?" She swung around to face him and found herself looking into his eyes. He was risking a lot to help her. No amount of money was worth his life. She wanted to tell him that he should leave her there and go back home. That she could figure things out and find a way back to Boston, but she had no money, no transportation and no way to get out of town.

She slid out of his coat and thrust it into his chest. "Better put this on. It's cold, and if you become hypothermic, we'll both be in trouble."

"The shed isn't heated."

"You're risking your life for me, Mac. Take the coat. Lock me in. Let's get this done." She stepped into the shed, refusing to think about whatever creature had been scurrying through the dark.

Mac studied her face, his gaze touching hers, then drifting down to her running gear. Running tights. Compression top. Jacket. "I'll be back as quickly as I can," he murmured, tugging the hood of her jacket over her head and tucking strands of hair inside, his fingers sliding across her cheek as his hand slipped away.

"Be careful," she whispered.

He nodded and shut the door, closing her into the dark shed. The chain rattled. The lock snapped home. She thought she heard his footsteps as he left, but it might have been her imagination.

Mac didn't enter rooms or leave loudly. He moved nearly silently. She had noticed that the same way she had noticed his gruff kindness, his concern for clients and for employees, his focus on the ranch, on the cattle, on his work. He didn't announce his presence when he entered a room the way some men did. The way Gabe had.

She frowned, pushing thoughts of her ex-husband away.

The marriage had ended three years ago.

She hadn't wasted time mourning it or wondering if her ex was happy with the woman he had left her for.

"You have way more important things to do than think about Gabe," she muttered.

At the sound of her voice, the thing in the shed scurried through the darkness, the rustling of dry leaves making her wonder if there were a nest of critters someone.

"Listen," she said. "I'm not here to evict you. I just want to share the space for a little while. We'll keep a few feet between us, and we'll both be happy. Okay?"

No more scurrying noises. No squeaks. No rodent feet clawing up her leg.

Her eyes adjusted to the dark, and she could make out shadowy tools. A riding lawn mower. A rake. A shovel. There were paint buckets stacked near one wall. A trashcan near another. A window on the wall looked out into thick hedges that had probably once been trimmed and cared for. Now they were overgrown, their branches butting up against the glass. She unlocked the window and wiggled it, testing to see if it would open. The last thing she wanted was to be trapped, if he didn't return.

But he would.

He had to.

She didn't want more regrets. She didn't want to spend more sleepless nights wondering if she could have done something different. If she could have tried harder. If she could have saved him.

"Keep him safe," she whispered, wondering if God would listen and respond. Since her divorce, she had spent more time working than worshiping. As a child and young adult, her faith had been unshakable. She had needed God to help her through the tough times with her mother. She had met Gabe in law school, two years after her mother's suicide. She had still been grieving, still been wracked with guilt for not being there when Sheila needed her most. Gabe had given her something to focus on. Serious and driven with undeniable charm, he had been the guy every girl in law school wanted. Annalise had felt privileged that he chose her.

They had married after graduation, taken

the bar exam on the same day, celebrated their passing scores, their new jobs, their courtroom wins. For two years, she had been certain that God had blessed her with an amazing life to make up for the difficult one she'd had as a child. Gabe had cooked dinners and brought flowers and treated her like she was the only woman in the world.

He probably would have continued to do that for the rest of their lives if she hadn't returned home for lunch on a particularly stressful day and found him with another woman.

She had forgiven him, of course. She had been set to live happily ever after, but even in that, she had known there would be bumps in the road. She had understood his busy schedule and his focus on his career. She had wanted children. He had wanted to wait. He had dreamed of practicing law in a city like New York or Las Vegas. A place with lights and glitz and glamour. She had liked the familiarity of Boston.

She had made efforts to appease him. She had stopped talking about kids and looked for jobs in other cities, but her heart wasn't in any of it. She wasn't sure her heart had been in the marriage.

Gabe's certainly hadn't been. After three years of marriage, he had announced that he had fallen in love with another woman. Annalise had known her. Allie was a paralegal who had worked with Gabe. The two had spent hours together on the weekends and after hours, prepping for trials and doing research for cases. If she had been paying more attention or been more interested in what he was doing, Annalise probably would have suspected the affair long before Gabe had announced it.

She probably should have been heartbroken, but she had felt relief more than anything.

He had moved out, filed for divorce, and moved on.

She had poured herself into her job, spending long weekends prepping for trials, foregoing church to catch a few hours of sleep. Sundays had become just another day to work, and she hadn't even realized it had happened until she had arrived at Sweet Valley Ranch and been forced to slow down, to breathe, and to think. She had spent the first few weeks getting used to the easy pace of life on the ranch. Once she had settled in, she had begun to think about how busy things had been in Boston, how hectic her life had often felt and how much she missed the connection to God that came with quiet moments spent in prayer.

She had never lost her faith or stopped praying, but her prayer time had often been rushed. A quick request for guidance as she ran through her day.

Now, every Sunday when she went to church with other ranch employees, she realized how far she had drifted from the faith-filled woman she had once been.

The window held tight, and she put muscle into it, breathing a sigh of relief as it inched up. If she had to, she could get out. She was hoping she wouldn't have to. She wanted things to go as Mac planned. He would get to the sheriff and bring help back to her. There would be no more gunfire. No men lunging at her from the shadows.

She shuddered, closing the window and retreating to the door. This wasn't what she had pictured when she'd agreed to enter Witness Protection. Maybe she had been naive, but it had never occurred to her that she wouldn't be safe. There were fail-safes in place to keep the program secure. There was no way anyone should have known that she was at Sweet Valley Ranch. She hadn't contacted anyone from her old life. She didn't have family that would worry about her. There had been no temptation to reach out and let people know that she was okay. She had friends, of course, but not the kind that would pace a hospital room waiting if she were badly injured.

She frowned, skirting the old lawn mower and searching the shed for a weapon and a hiding place. If she and Mac had been able to break into the shed, other people could do the same. She needed to be prepared.

Other people? Assassins. That's what they are, and you need to face up to that and deal with it.

She could almost hear Sheila's raspy smoker's voice and the frenetic tap of her fingers on her thighs. She had had her problems, but she had been the best mother she knew how to be. She had tried to give Annalise what she hadn't had herself—stability and love, security and affection. If she had lived, Annalise would have made good on the promise she had once made her—to buy her a little house near a lake. A quiet retreat where she could live her life away from the rushing madness of Boston life.

She had been going to college, planning her future and her mother's when she had received news of her Sheila's death. A suicide that had surprised even her psychiatrist, it had left a hole in Annalise's heart and her life.

And it had left her feeling guilty.

Guilt on top of guilt on top of guilt.

That seemed to be the story of her life.

"Part of the story," she reminded herself as she picked her way across the small shed, lifting old burlap bags, hoping to find a pitchfork, shovel, rake. Ax. Anything that she might be able to use to defend herself.

She wanted to get through this.

She wanted to testify and go back to her life.

Whatever was left of it when this was over.

She tried not to think about giant rats or men with guns. She tried not to imagine Mac ambushed, bleeding, dying on the ground.

He was strong.

He was tough.

He was smart.

He wouldn't allow himself to be overtaken.

He would return.

They would escape.

She would make it back to Boston for the trial.

That was what she needed to focus on. It was what she needed to believe.

Aside from the riding mower and garden tools that were rusty or broken, there wasn't much in the shed. No boxes. Nothing to hide behind if trouble came. Except the trashcan. She lifted the lid. It was empty. She could fit inside if she needed to. She replaced the lid and glanced up. There was a small loft, but no ladder to access it. She stood on tiptoe and reached for the edge, her fingers barely grazing it. She dragged the trashcan over, tipped it upside down and climbed onto it, hoisting herself up and scrambling onto the plywood floor. She couldn't stand, so she crawled, easing in between boxes that she hoped were filled with something she could use to protect herself.

She opened one, telling herself she wasn't going to find a rat's nest or a bed of finger-nipping mice. She found file folders filled with papers, a few books and a framed photograph of a couple on their wedding day. She opened a second box and a third with the same results. Plenty of paper. Nothing that would be useful in defending herself. There were several boxes shoved against the shed's eaves. She reached for one, sliding it toward her, the soft scuffing sound mixing with another sound. She stopped pulling and listened, her heartbeat ratcheting up as the murmur of voices drifted into the shed.

She froze, her heart thudding painfully in her chest.

Someone was coming.

She eased backward away from the edge, shimmying behind boxes, hoping she was completely hidden from anyone who might look in the window. The chain rattled, the door squeaking as someone attempted to open it. Not Mac. He hadn't had time to get to the sheriff's and back.

"Kick it in," a man said, the words clear as day and filling her with dread. If they entered, they'd find her. The trashcan below was a dead giveaway to what she'd done and where she was.

"Kick it in and wake up the neighborhood? I don't think so," another man responded. The voice sounded familiar. Not someone from her old life. There was a Southern drawl rather than a Boston accent.

"What neighborhood? This place is in the middle of nowhere."

"It only looks that way. Go past those trees and there are plenty of homes. And sound travels far in places like this. Someone will hear. The cops will be called. Next thing you know, we're in jail."

"Only if they catch us." The chain rattled again.

Annalise tensed, expecting the door to

crash in and light to illuminate her hiding spot.

"Our transportation is back near the ranch. Since everyone in this town is home and in bed before ten most nights, it'll be pretty easy for the sheriff and his deputies to find us," the second man argued. "Besides, the door is locked and has been forever. Look at the rust on it. Do you really think she ducked in there, then somehow managed to lock an exterior lock?"

"If I didn't know better, I'd think you were trying to keep me from checking the shed," the first man growled, rattling the lock again.

"I'm trying to keep us from getting caught. We don't get paid unless she's gone. And she won't be gone if we end up in jail."

"You've got a point, but I still want to check this place. Maybe there's another entrance."

"There's a window."

"You know an awful lot about this little town and this property, don't you?"

"In a town this size, that's not difficult."

"Where's the window?"

"Around the side."

They men fell silent, the sound of feet crunching dead leaves and winter-dry grass muted but audible.

Annalise counted their steps, her heart in her throat, her mind racing. She'd left the trashcan in the middle of the shed, the lid on the floor beside it. She had no idea who either man was, but one seemed to know everything there was to know about her hiding spot.

Did he know where the trashcan had been?

Would he realize it had been moved?

Light flashed near the window.

She held her breath, watching as the soft glow brightened. A beam of light speared through the window. She ducked, wanting to watch, but afraid the light would find her.

"I told you she wasn't in there," one of the men muttered. "Even if she had managed to get the door open—"

"We aren't just talking about her," the first man spat. "We're talking about MacArthur Davis. From the intel I've got on him, it looks like he knows how to take care of himself and everyone around him. A guy like him could easily pick a lock and enter a shed."

"A guy like Mac would be way too smart to back himself in a corner. And that's what he'd be doing if he were in the shed."

"All the more reason to take him out. We're being paid for the woman, but he's standing in our way. Let's check out the church."

"It's locked."

"I said, we're checking it out."

The second man said something Annalise couldn't hear. She waited as the conversation faded, then lowered onto the floor. She left the trashcan where it was, eased open the window and climbed out. She closed it carefully, listening for voices, her pulse swooshing loudly in her ears.

She had told Mac she would stay where he had left her.

But that was before she had realized the men who were after her also planned to kill him.

She had to warn him.

She couldn't allow him to be hurt or killed because of her.

She knew the way to the sheriff's office. If she sprinted, she could make it there before the hit men caught up.

She glanced at the church. Both men were there, silhouetted by the outdoor lights. They were moving away, rounding the side of the building and disappearing. She ran in the opposite direction, crossing a small field and sprinting onto the road. Her feet pounded pavement, her frozen toes burning as blood circulated into her extremities.

She passed a crossroad and another, turned down Main Street and kept going.

There were plenty of businesses around. All of them were closed. Even if they hadn't been, even if the sidewalk had been overflowing with pedestrians, she wouldn't have felt safe. Witnessing the cold-blooded murder of two men had made her very aware of how fragile life was and how quickly things could change from good to bad. Moreno's henchman, Reginald Boeing, hadn't cared if he was seen. He hadn't been worried about being tried and convicted of murder. More than likely, he had planned to kill everyone standing on the courthouse steps that night. He had failed, but Archie Moreno had more money than Midas, and he knew how to use it to get what he wanted.

He wanted Annalise dead.

She had seen Reginald's face. She had known exactly who he was from news reports on other murders that he was suspected in. Even if she hadn't seen the reports, she would have known him. She had come face to face with him a few times in her work, and she had recognized him immediately. It had taken a few seconds longer to realize he was holding a gun, pointing it out the window of the vehicle he was riding in.

It was only after the shooting, that she realized why he had been there and why he had opened fire. The prosecuting attorneys working the shooting investigation against Reginald could easily link him with Moreno through phone records. The FBI had extensive surveillance video of the mob boss and Reginald meeting. Reginald had been on their radar for years, suspected of several murders that the FBI was certain Moreno had paid for. There had been no proof, though. No evidence. Nothing to tie Reginald to the crimes he was suspected of.

Until the courthouse shooting.

Thomas Ryland, Moreno's second-in-command, had known too much about the inner workings of the business. He had been willing to talk for the right plea deal, and Moreno had needed to make certain that didn't happen. If Annalise hadn't witnessed the shooting, he would have walked away again.

Now the only thing standing between Moreno and freedom was Annalise and her testimony. She had seen Reginald Boeing fire the shots that had killed two men. Until now, no case against Moreno had ever been successful. She wanted to make certain this one was. Once Boeing was convicted, then Moreno would be tried for solicitation of murder. That, along with other charges the prosecuting attorney had filed, would put him away for life.

She needed to return to Boston safely so that she could testify in the trial. But first, she needed to let Mac know that the hit men who were after her knew who he was, and that they were after him too.

Mac had known Sheriff River Williams for almost as long as either of them had been alive. They had met as grade school kids, both visiting family for the summer. Mac had been at the ranch. River had been at his grandmother's farm just outside of the town. Mac had gone home after the summer. River had stayed for reasons he had never explained to anyone. Mac had been certain that River would return to his hometown of Houston once he graduated high school, but River had stayed. He'd followed his Aunt Bonnie's footsteps and gone into law enforcement. Three years ago, he had become the town's youngest sheriff. He took the job seriously. He took the town and the people in it seriously. He kept his cruiser spotless, his uniform pressed and his shoes shined. He also kept the crime rate down and communication between the small town and its law enforcement officers open.

Right now, he was sitting behind the wheel of his marked sheriff's car, looking at Mac as if he had grown two heads and a tail.

"You're trying to tell me that you've got

the witness to a high-profile case hiding out on your ranch?" he asked, raising a dark brow and staring straight into Mac's eyes.

"I *had* one hiding on my ranch. Right now, she's in a shed on the old church property on the edge of town." He hoped. It had taken Mac longer than he would have liked to track down River. He hadn't been in his office, and Mac hadn't wanted to ask the dispatcher to locate him. He had no idea who was involved in leaking the information about Anna. Until he did, he was going to trust very few people.

River eyed him silently.

"If you're waiting for more information, that's all I've got," Mac said impatiently, the cold seeping through his jeans and coat and wrapping him in a viselike grip that made his bones ache.

"I'm trying to figure out why you would allow someone who could bring danger on your property," River replied.

"How about we discuss that after she's safe?" he suggested.

"All right. Hop in." He motioned for Mac to climb in the front passenger seat, then accelerated, speeding through the backroads of town and onto the main thoroughfare that led past the sheriff's office and back to the church. They rounded a curve in the road and the headlights caught the quick movement of a shadow darting behind thick hedges.

"Did you see that?" Mac asked.

"Yes." River coasted to the curb and braked. "Stay here. I'll check it out."

"How about we both check it out. These guys mean business, River. I don't think they're worried about shooting a police officer."

"I'm wearing body armor. Are you?" River exited the vehicle and jogged to the hedges.

Mac followed, making sure to stay out of River's line of fire. The moon had disappeared behind heavy clouds. The air was thick with moisture. Streetlights gleamed on asphalt and cement, the glow from porch lights shining on well-tended yards. Something rustled in the hedges as they approached. Someone was sliding through the foliage.

"Sheriff's department, come out of there. Now. Hands where I can see them!" River commanded, his gun drawn and pointed at the hedges.

"I'm trying," a woman replied.

A woman whose voice Mac recognized!

"Anna?" He hurried forward, peering under the shrubs. She was there, her hair wound so tightly in the branches, she could barely move her head.

"What happened?" he asked.

"I saw headlights. I was worried. I ducked for cover, and I didn't realize the thing I was ducking behind had thorns," she replied. "Now that I've explained, can you get me out of here? The guys who were chasing us were at the church. They tried to get in the shed."

"And that made you think it would be a good idea to leave a safe spot and run for it?" he muttered, reaching into the thorny hedge and gently untangling her hair.

"Everything okay?" River asked, crouching next to him.

"If you call being chased by men who want you dead okay, then yes. Everything is fine," Anna replied as she crawled out and got to her feet. "I know one of them. Or I've met him," she said without preamble.

"The men at the church?" Mac asked, his gaze shifting from her pale face to the empty road. If she was being pursued, the men were too far back to be seen. Or too well hidden. He stepped between her and the asphalt.

"Yes, and they know who you are."

"That's not surprising."

"From what I heard, they plan to get rid of you when they get rid of me."

"Also not surprising."

"How about we talk about this in my office?" River asked, taking Anna's arm and leading her to his cruiser. He motioned for her to climb in the passenger seat. "Sorry, Mac. You get a backseat ride."

"It's not like I haven't been there before," he responded, waiting impatiently for him to open the door. He had more questions. Lots of them.

He slid into the back seat of the cruiser.

"You've been in the back seat of a cruiser before?" Anna had twisted in her seat so she could look at him through the fiber-glass partition.

"A friend and I decided to trespass on state property. We got caught. The security guard thought he would teach us a lesson by calling the police."

"I was the friend," River said as he pulled away from the curb.

"What'd you do? Break into a zoo?"

"There's no zoo out here, ma'am," River replied, offering a quick smile that Mac recognized from their teenage years. He obviously found Anna attractive. Who wouldn't? She had a natural beauty that was impossible not to notice. Silky hair. Smooth skin. High cheekbones. She had freckles, too. Across her nose and sprinkled on her cheeks.

"A state park?" she asked, her gaze focused on the street behind them.

"Briarwood State Hospital. It was a place people were sent when they had tuberculous. Later it was a home for unwed mothers and then eventually it was a home for troubled youth. That was shut down, and it's been abandoned since."

"I'm surprised I've never seen it," she said, but Mac doubted she was invested in the conversation. She was more concerned with what might be coming up behind them.

"You said you recognized one of the men?" He cut in, and she met his eyes.

"I didn't see them, but one of them had a familiar voice."

"Familiar from Boston?" he asked, hoping that it was. He didn't want to believe that anyone from the ranch or from Briarwood would betray him.

"No. It was someone I met here."

"You're sure?" River frowned, his relaxed good-old-boy facade gone.

"There is a big difference between a Boston accent and a Texas drawl," she replied.

"There are people from Texas everywhere, ma'am," River reminded her.

"And people from Boston everywhere, but I haven't met anyone here with a Boston accent. And I don't know anyone in Boston who has a Texas drawl," she responded.

"All right. We'll assume the person is someone you met here. Any idea who?"

"No, but if I heard him speak, I'd probably know it was him."

"I guess we can start this investigation by bringing in potential suspects for questioning. You can listen in."

"We're not going to be here long enough for that," Mac said as River pulled into the small parking area near the sheriff's department and stopped the cruiser near a back door.

"You came to me for help, Mac. I'm going to give it, but this is an open investigation until I close it, and I'm going to need full cooperation from you and from Ms...?"

"Meade. Anna." She gave her alias rather than her real identity.

"Until I complete the investigation and arrest the people responsible, I'm going to have to ask you both to stay in town."

"You can ask all you want, but that doesn't mean we're staying," Mac responded.

He explained the situation in detail. The federal case. The dead prosecuting attorney and state's witness. Three survivors and only one who had seen the shooter.

"We're friends, Mac, but I'm a law enforcement officer before I'm anything. If there are hit men wandering around my town, it's my job to find them and toss them in jail. Ms. Meade says she recognized a voice. We can have suspects in here within minutes, and we can start the identification process. If you want to give your statement and go home, feel free. But she's staying."

River got out of the cruiser and rounded the vehicle, opening the door for Anna and taking her arm.

For a split second, Mac wondered if River would leave him in the cruiser. There were no door handles. No interior locks. Nothing that would enable him to escape. That thought brought a darker one. Was River involved in the plot against Anna?

The door opened, and he climbed out. On edge. Frustrated with himself. He had been in a situation that could have easily been used against him and Anna. The glass in the cruiser was bulletproof. The car was made to keep people from escaping. He could have been trapped there. Anna could have been killed.

He had known River for nearly three decades. They had been friends for most of their lives, but close friends could betray you. People you trusted could stab you in the back. He had seen it. He had lived it. He had broken off an engagement to his high school sweetheart because she had cheated with the person he had chosen as his best man. They had been days from getting married. The venue had been picked, the cake made, the tuxes ordered. He'd had every intention of saying *I do*. Even though he had had doubts. Even though he had wondered if they could make it forever. He had loved Sydney, but they had gotten engaged before he went to basic training. They had stayed engaged as he passed SEAL training and entered the service. He had returned to his hometown when he could, spending time with her and planning their wedding. The more he had grown, the more he had learned about life, the less sure he was that they had enough in common to sustain a life together.

But he had never imagined that she would betray him.

He hadn't been prepared to hear that the person she had betrayed him with was his best childhood friend.

The experience hadn't broken his heart— he had been relieved to have a reason to not go through with the wedding—but it had taught him a valuable lesson. Everyone had secrets. Sometimes those secrets were dark and painful and ugly.

He took Anna's arm.

He could see the concern in her face, the hint of tension at the corners of her mouth, the tightness in her jaw and neck. Their plans had been waylaid by a supposedly well-meaning law enforcement officer. Until River said different, they were stuck in town.

Unless they made a run for it.

And if they had a chance, that was exactly what Mac planned to do. Until he knew who had betrayed them, he wouldn't trust anyone.

"It's going to be okay," he said.

"Maybe," she replied as they walked into

the old brick building that housed the sheriff's office.

"It will be," he assured her.

He planned to make certain of it.

Protecting Anna had been an assignment. Something he had done for the sake of the ranch his grandfather had loved.

Now it was personal.

He would find a way to get her out of town, and they would stay hidden until he knew exactly who they could trust and who they couldn't.

FIVE

The sheriff's department was as quaint as the town, the two-story building filled with old wood and narrow halls. Annalise followed the sheriff through one of them, Mac's hand cupping her elbow. He hadn't let go of her since he'd gotten out of the police cruiser. She hadn't pulled away. Maybe it had occurred to him, as it had to her, that the sheriff might not let him out of the cruiser. That she might be ushered into the building, locked up and found dead the next morning. A suicide or heart attack caused by an untraceable drug.

She shivered, the heat doing little to chase away the cold that had settled deep in her bones.

"Go ahead and have a seat, Ms. Meade,"

the sheriff said, his dark eyes staring straight into hers. She had seen him in town a few times. He didn't seem to embody the small-town pace that most people in Briarwood embraced. He moved more quickly. Spoke faster and with less of an accent. She wouldn't say he seemed to be in a hurry, but he never seemed to be taking his time, moving through the world at a leisurely pace. She wondered if he had dreams of leaving Briarwood and becoming a big city police officer. He would fit well in a place like Boston.

"You, too, Mac," he directed as he rounded an ancient desk and sat in a new leather chair. The room was large, with two windows flanked by floor-to-ceiling bookshelves. On another wall, file cabinets stood side by side.

She grabbed one of the straight-back chairs that stood near the door and pulled it over, taking a seat so quickly she thought its spindly legs might give out under her weight.

"I need to make a couple of phone calls, River. I can step out in the hall to do it," Mac replied. In the harsh overhead light, his hair was a mix of burnished copper and chestnut brown, his eyes silvery blue, fine lines fanning out from them. She had watched him work with dude ranch visitors. She had seen him running cattle. She couldn't remember ever seeing him stand still. Even now, he was fidgeting, flipping his cell phone over and over in his hand.

"How about you do that after we talk? I want to get a better handle on what's going on here and then send some of my deputies out looking for our perps."

"You might want to send them out now. You have armed men wandering through town. I don't have to tell you that's a dangerous situation."

"You're right. It's a dangerous situation, and I don't need to be told." The sheriff frowned and stood. "I'm going to dispatch a couple deputies to search for our perps. Any physical description you can give?"

"I didn't see them," Anna responded.

"How about you, Mac?"

"I wish I had something to offer you. It was dark, and we were running. I couldn't see any details."

"They were on foot? Or in a vehicle?"

"On foot when they were at the church," Anna said. "I heard one of them mention their vehicle being parked near the ranch."

"I saw a vehicle. It was a late model Ford Explorer. Black or dark blue. The license plate was covered, so I couldn't even get a partial."

The sheriff's eyes lit up, and he smiled. "That's something to go on, at least. You two stay here. I'll be back soon."

He stepped out into the hall and closed the door.

Mac pulled a chair over and sat, his shoulder brushing Anna's. He was close enough that she could feel the chill radiating from the exterior of his coat. He took it off, dropped it around her shoulders without offering, asking or commenting.

She didn't protest.

She wanted to get this meeting over with and get on the next plane back to Boston. The way she saw it, if her cover had been blown and her hiding place revealed, she might as well be back at her apartment, tucked away behind locked doors and shaded windows.

She had no idea who she could trust.

Aside from Mac, it was possible anyone was the enemy. Even the sheriff. She eyed the closed door, wondering if he was really sending deputies out or if he were calling Moreno.

"What are you thinking?" Mac asked.

"That I feel like a sitting duck. I have no idea who told Moreno I was here, and I have no idea who I can trust."

"You're wondering about the sheriff?"

"Aren't you?"

"I wish I could say no. We've been friends for years."

"But, you can't?"

"I don't want to take chances with your

life. Not even slim ones. Come on. Let's get out of here." Mac grabbed her hand and pulled her from the chair. He pulled the curtains back from one of the windows. "The great thing about the old buildings in this town is that most of them don't have modern locks."

"I'd think a sheriff's office would."

"In the more modern part of the building, it does. Here, things are just the way they were a century ago." He unlocked the window and opened it. "Come on. Let's get out of here."

"And go where? We've already got murderers chasing us. If we climb out this window, we'll have the sheriff and his deputies after us, too."

"We haven't done anything wrong. River will come looking for us, but he's not going to arrest us for leaving."

"Then, why don't we just walk out the same way we walked in?" she asked. She knew he was right. They hadn't committed a crime but climbing out the window would make her feel like they were running from the law.

"I don't want to believe River is involved in giving our location to Moreno. I don't think he would do something like that, but I don't want to take chances. I want to leave, and I don't want to be followed."

"So, we climb out the window and go where?"

"My grandfather owned a hunting cabin twenty miles from town. We're going there."

"On foot?"

"I'll get us a ride."

"From?"

"How about we get out of here and then I'll explain."

"I'd rather know the entire plan first," she muttered.

"If I take the time to explain, we may lose our opportunity to leave."

"If we move forward on a plan that isn't going to work—" she began.

"My grandfather always used to say that

a mediocre plan with great follow-through is better than a great plan with no follow-through." He had the window open and the screen off. All she had to do was climb out, and they'd be on their way to freedom.

Or danger.

Maybe both.

But Mac was right. Enacting a plan of action that was only partially thought through was better than thinking up a better plan and never having the chance to implement it.

She climbed out, stepping into an alley between the sheriff's department and the town's pharmacy. Not a big-name place. Just a small family-owned business where people in town came to get their prescriptions filled.

Mac was right on her heels, grabbing her arm as he exited the building and holding it as he closed the window and replaced the screen.

"You don't have to hold on to me, Mac. It's not like I'm going to run off," she told him.

"Maybe not, but I don't believe in taking chances."

"What chances? We're standing inches from each other," she whispered, worried that her voice would carry into the building and a half-dozen deputy sheriffs would come running to apprehend them.

"You told me you'd stay in the shed. You didn't."

"I was worried about *you*. That's why I left. I needed to warn you that they were gunning for both of us."

"I appreciate the sentiment, but it could have gotten you killed."

"It didn't," she pointed out as they hurried through the alley and out into the sheriff's department parking lot. There were three cars there. Two of them marked cruisers. She hadn't had much of a chance to get to know the local law enforcement, but she didn't think there were more than a few full-time deputies. Briarwood was small. Maybe a couple thousand full-time residents.

"That doesn't change the facts. You said you would stay in the shed. You didn't."

"So you're going to hold on to my arm for however long it takes for us to get to safety?"

"At the moment, that's the plan." He was moving quickly. Not running, but not out for a leisurely stroll. She had no idea where they were heading. If Mac did, he wasn't saying.

Thick clouds shrouded the moon, and the cool air had turned damp with coming rain or snow. She tried to imagine walking or running twenty miles to the cabin Mac mentioned. She couldn't. She had always believed that a positive mental attitude, a plan of action and faith could get her through anything. She wasn't sure they would get her through this. Already exhausted, still cold from her time outside, she didn't know how long she could continue moving forward. Mac had said they would get a ride, but so far, all they were doing was rushing somewhere on foot.

They skirted past the Main Street businesses and turned down a side road with fewer houses, all of them old and stately. Farmhouse style, Greek Revival and a few Victorians stood on large, well-manicured lots.

"Do you really think we're going to get to your grandfather's cabin?" she asked, her voice hollow with fatigue and fear. They could be walking straight into the paths of the assassins Moreno had sent. The thought terrified her.

"Yes."

"Before we run into Moreno's thugs?"

"That's the plan."

"And, if we don't manage to avoid them?"

"We'll cross that bridge—"

"When we come to it." She completed the thought. "But, I'd rather not come to it. Do you have a plan to avoid being seen until we get that ride you were talking about?"

"We're going somewhere warm where I

can make a phone call." His hand moved from her arm to her back as he ushered her into a driveway that led to a two-story farmhouse. The lawn was trimmed and tidy, an old elm standing sentinel in the center of a lush lawn. A tire swing hung from its branches, still and listless despite the cold breeze.

"Whose place is this?" she whispered as they walked around the side of the house. A privacy fence separated them from the backyard. Six feet tall and solid, it prevented any glimpse of what lay beyond.

"An old friend of my father's owned it. They grew up together. My dad moved to Houston. The friend stayed behind. He married and had a daughter. His wife left and took the little girl with her. That was twenty-five years ago. He spent thousands of hours and thousands of dollars trying to find her, but he never saw her again."

"That's terrible."

"It is. He spent every day hoping and praying his daughter would find her way back. He died of cancer two years ago, still hoping."

"That's even worse," she said, her heart breaking at the thought of a father spending his days longing for his child to return.

"It was. It is," he agreed. "The house is to be kept in trust for her. If she returns, it's hers. For now, my father is the executor of the will, and he makes sure the property is maintained."

"Is he trying to find her?" she asked as he lifted a rock near the fence and grabbed the key that lay beneath it.

"Yes. Adam—his friend—wanted him to, but he didn't want her to be pressured to accept her inheritance. He said that if his daughter lived in the family home, it should be because she wanted to. Not because she felt obligated. Briarwood isn't for everyone. He knew that." He reached over the gate and unlocked it, swinging it open and hurrying Anna into the yard. He relocked the gate and shoved the key in his pocket. "Come on."

"Where?"

"Inside."

"But..."

"We don't have time to argue. River has probably already put out an APB on us. He knows my father is keeping up this place, and it isn't going to take him long to get over here."

"We shouldn't be here when he arrives," she hissed, following him up the stairs that led to a door.

"He won't know we're here if everything is locked up tight and the lights are off. Without probable cause, he can't enter the premises without permission or a warrant." He pulled a multitool from his pocket and picked the lock the same way he had at the shed.

She stepped inside, expecting it to be cold and empty. The heat was on, the warmth so welcome she nearly collapsed in a heap on the floor. "The furnace is running," she whispered as if there were someone else in the house who might hear them.

"Old houses do better if they're not left to the capriciousness of the weather. There's a trust set up to keep the electricity and the heat on and to do whatever maintenance is necessary." He led her through a nice-sized kitchen and into a hallway. He didn't turn on the lights, but she could see the front door and the living room, its windows with a view of the yard. She thought a dining room was on the other side of center stairs that curved up to the second floor.

"Look," Mac said, pointing to the windows. Blue lights flashed on the street as a police car rolled to a stop in front of the house. "This way." He yanked her sideways, opening a hallway door and closing it quickly behind them.

Mac had known it wouldn't take River long to realize they were gone and to come up with places where they might be hiding. He could only hope they hadn't left any sign that they were here at the house. He had tried to walk on the driveway and avoid leaving footprints in the grass, but River was good at his job. If they had left a trail, he would find it.

"Do you think he knows we're here?" Anna whispered.

"Maybe. He won't come in without permission, though."

"Couldn't he call your father and ask permission?"

"He could." He probably would, and knowing his father, Mac was certain River would be given the permission he needed.

"Maybe you should call your father and tell him not to allow it."

"I'm not pulling my father into this. Even if I wanted to, and I don't, refusing to allow River to enter the house would only make him suspicious, and that would probably be enough reason to obtain a warrant."

"So, what's the plan?"

"Make my phone call. Get out before River reaches my father." He took her arm.

"There are ten steps. Be careful, okay? If you fall and get injured, we'll have to turn ourselves in and hope that River is on our side."

"It would be easier to be careful if there was a light," she muttered. He could hear her hand sliding against the wall. He had been in the house several times, checking on it for his father. There was no railing on the basement stairs and the floor below was cement. He held on to Anna's elbow as they made their way through the darkness. When they reached the bottom, he pulled out his phone and dialed the number Daniel Avery had given him for emergencies.

Daniel picked up immediately, his voice taut with concern. "What's wrong?"

"We ran into some trouble."

"You and my witness?"

"Yes."

"How?"

"That's a good question. I'll give you an answer as soon as I have one."

"Where are you?"

"I'd rather not say."

"What do you mean, you'd rather not say?" Daniel's voice rose a notch, his frustration obvious.

"There's a leak. There is no other way Anna could have been found. Until I know who the leak is, I'm taking full responsibility for getting her to trial."

"What's that supposed to mean?"

"It means, I'll keep you posted on her well-being, but for now, I'm not telling anyone where we are."

"Is this a game, MacArthur? A joke? If it is, I'm not amused."

"No game. I suggest you start looking at your organization and the people who knew where Anna was hiding."

"I suggest—"

Mac disconnected and dialed a second number, his focus half on the ringing phone and half on the silence of the house. Anna, for once, wasn't talking, her quiet breathing the only indication that she was still standing nearby. If River entered the house, Mac would hear it. There was a cellar door that led into the side yard. If he heard a door open, they'd be outside before River searched the basement.

"Hello?" Linda's gruff voice filled his ear, a smoker's rasp still apparent even though she had quit five years ago. The owner of a used car lot just outside of the city limits, she had been a fixture in town for as long as Mac had been there.

"Linda, it's Mac. I need a ride." He didn't say why. He knew she wouldn't ask. She was the kind of person who helped the people she cared about without asking questions or expecting repayment.

"What kind?"

"Anything that works."

"Well, kid, I've got a bunch of keys in my office at the shop. They're all labeled. You shouldn't have any trouble finding a vehicle you can use. The security code is 7346. Spare key taped to the underside of the dumpster behind the shop. Left side of it. You take what you want off the lot. No questions asked."

"I appreciate it."

"Just bring it back unharmed. If you don't, you'll owe me."

"I'll pay for the damage."

"Ha! Forget that. I've got more used cars on that lot than I know what to do with. You'll owe me a date, young man. It's been too long since we've seen each other. I want to hear how your folks are doing."

"You've got it. Whether the vehicle is damaged or not."

"You need a ride to the lot?" she asked. Linda usually didn't ask many questions. She'd seen her share of hard times, and she wasn't the kind of person to judge others for theirs. Tough and hard-edged, she had a soft side that most people in Briarwood knew about but no one ever mentioned. Linda preferred to think she was viewed as a crotchety old woman.

"No. And do me a favor, don't mention this call to anyone. If you're asked,

I wanted a ride out of town. You weren't able to give me one."

"What kind of trouble are you in, kid?"

"Not the kind you need to worry about. I'll call you in a few days. We'll meet for lunch." He disconnected and set the phone on the floor. He had no doubt his cell phone would be pinged and used to locate him. River might not be able to get a warrant to do it quickly, but Daniel would. He had plenty of connections and a lot riding on making certain Anna made it to trial.

"What now?" Anna asked, her voice shaking. He could see her face through the darkness, her eyes shadowed, her skin pale.

"Are you okay?" He touched her forehead, feeling for fever or icy skin. It was cool in the basement, but warm enough that she shouldn't be shaking.

"I'm cold. I'm tired. I'm scared. Other than that, I'm great," she responded truthfully. "I want this over, Mac. I want to go back to the life I had before I witnessed the courthouse shooting."

"It will happen."

"I hope so. I worked hard to have a nice stable predictable life. I shouldn't be in a situation like this."

He understood her thoughts. He knew how it felt to have the rug pulled out from under neat plans and grand goals. He hadn't intended to be a rancher. He had intended to travel the world. To explore. To use the military as a vehicle to serve his country and to satisfy his wanderlust.

The medical discharge he'd received had changed those plans. The fact that his grandfather had mortgaged the ranch had sent Mac in new directions that he never would have expected or wanted when he was young.

He had no regrets.

But, there wasn't time to talk about God's plans, His will or the way that bad things often turned out for the good.

"You'll get your life back, Anna," he assured her.

"I hope so," she responded.

He was tempted to pull her into his arms and offer a comforting hug, but there wasn't time for that, either.

"Come on." He tugged her to the cellar exit and walked up the few steps to the hatch-style door, unlocking it quickly. Refusing to doubt his plan. Refusing to second-guess it. For now, relying on his instincts made more sense than relying on anything else.

"What if they're outside waiting?"

"What if they're not?"

"I'm too tired for games, Mac," she said wearily.

"I was making a statement. I can say it another way if you'd like."

"I know what you were getting at. We could stand here all night with nothing on the other side of the door to stop us. Except our fear."

"Exactly."

"Fine. You've made your point. Let's get it over with."

"That's the spirit," he said, and she snorted.

"My spirit is just about done for the night. I hope the sheriff isn't involved in leaking my location to Moreno, but if he isn't, he's not going to be happy that we're doing this."

"He'll understand. I know him well enough to know that he would do the same if he were in my position."

"You're sure?"

"Yes. My first obligation is to you. Until I know who is involved in this, I'm not trusting anyone here in town. He'll understand that."

"I hope you're right. Let's go." She started to push the cellar door open. He put a hand on her arm to stop her.

"Hold on. It's loud if it drops back into place. We have to be careful." He brushed her hand away, his fingers skimming over cool silky skin. Something flickered in his belly. That age-old acknowledgment that he was a man standing close to a beautiful woman. He ignored it, easing open the door and peering out into the side yard. There were trashcans and a recycle bin sitting on a wooden platform that stood between the cellar door and the street. He couldn't see beyond them, but there were no blue lights reflecting on the grass or the house. He opened the door enough to allow Anna to squeeze out. "I'll hold it, you go," he said. "Not far. Just out. Stay close and stay down. We don't want anyone to see us."

"No need for the warning. I'm very aware of the situation we're in," she whispered, sliding out on her belly and crouching inches away. She grabbed the edge of the door with both hands, opening it a few inches wider. She didn't speak, didn't move. Just waited as he eased out, took the door from her hands and gently lowered it back into place.

The neighbor's house was fifty meters

away, across a dark patch of grass that had clear view of the street.

"Stay down," he mouthed, lying on his belly and motioning for her to do the same. They army-crawled across the cleared area and into the neighbor's backyard. Once they were out of sight of the street, he stood and pulled her to her feet.

She leaned close, her lips touching his ear as she whispered, "What now?"

"We go find our ride," he replied, taking her hand and leading her across the unfenced yard. Most people in Briarwood didn't have security lights or alarm systems. In a town where everyone knew everyone, good intentions were presumed, and crime was rarely an issue. That would work to their advantage as they made their way across town to Linda's used car lot. Dogs were Mac's biggest concern as he cut through one yard after another, staying close to the buildings and deep in the shadows.

River's deputies were doing their jobs.

Mac counted three marked cruisers driving slowly through town. Each time, he and Anna stayed down and still and until the vehicle passed.

By the time they reached the end of the residential area, he was on edge, adrenaline coursing through him, his muscles tense. If he weren't careful, he would have a full-on panic attack. It had been years since he'd had one, but his time in the military hadn't left him unscathed. He had scars. Plenty of them on his body and even more on his soul. He had been in therapy. He had faced his troubles and, with the help of a therapist and his faith, had beat them back. They still came back to haunt him sometimes. He needed to keep moving, focus his mind, get to the car lot and get out of town, but sweat was suddenly beading his brow, and his hands shook as he shoved them in the pockets of his jeans.

"It's going to be okay," Anna said, touching his shoulder hesitantly, her palm just skimming his shirt before it settled lightly on his bicep.

"I know."

"You're shaking," she pointed out. No judgment. No question. Nothing in her voice but concern. He appreciated that, but he didn't have time to explain. He didn't want to explain. His time in the military was something he only discussed with the men and women he had served with.

"We all have our troubles, Anna. Even me. Come on. We're almost there." He lifted her hand from his arm, holding it gently as he stepped into sparse woods that separated the main part of town from the less affluent area. Linda lived in a small house near the car lot, its clapboard siding faded and gray with age and neglect. Most people in town never visited her there. She was known to have a hot temper and sharp tongue, but when she cared, she cared enough for twenty people.

He skirted around her property, staying in the woods until the lot was in front of them, the cars gleaming in the streetlights that illuminated it.

"What now?" Anna asked, her fingers curved through his as she scanned the lot.

"Linda said we can borrow a car," he replied, hurrying to the dumpster and running his hands along the underside until he found the key. He had the door open and the alarm off within seconds. A ring of car keys hung from a hook near Linda's desk, each one marked. He didn't spend a lot of time mulling over options. He could hear a clock ticking in his head, hurrying him along, reminding him that River wasn't stupid, that he would think about the used car lot and probably send a cruiser out to keep an eye on it.

He grabbed the key ring and thumbed through the keys and key fobs, sliding one after another along the cold metal ring until he removed one marked Ford Escort. 2014. Black.

"Let's go." He led her back outside, his

body humming with adrenaline, his mind shouting a warning.

Time was running out.

They needed to get off the lot and away from town.

Now.

He stopped near a small SUV. Maybe a few years old with a ding in the fender.

He pressed the button on the fob, and the doors unlocked.

"Get in," he commanded, opening the driver's door and nearly shoving Anna inside. She scrambled across the console, dropping into the seat and reaching for the belt. He heard it snap closed as he turned off the automatic headlights. There was no sense in announcing the fact that they were driving off the lot by having the lights on. He turned on the engine. It purred to life smoothly and effortlessly. He braced himself, expecting to see strobe lights, hear a police siren and a voice calling out for them to get out of the vehicle. The area remained dark, the road clear. If River was heading in their direction, he was doing it slowly.

Mac pulled onto the road, flicking on the windshield wipers as a few drops of rain splattered the glass.

"We did it," Anna breathed as the used car lot faded into the distance.

"We're not out of the woods yet," he responded, glancing in the rearview mirror as he neared a curve in the road. Headlights appeared and then disappeared, a lone car heading in their direction. River? A deputy? The hired hit men?

Or just someone from town out for a late-night drive?

"Actually, we are. And I will be forever grateful for that." She reached over and turned up the heat, holding her hands in front of the vent. They were shaking violently, her fingers blue-tinged from cold.

"You're nearly frozen," he muttered, turning the vents in her direction.

"I'll warm up soon enough." She leaned her head back against the seat and closed her eyes. "At least I don't have to worry about being shot while I'm doing it."

He glanced in the rearview mirror again, saw the lights in the distance, heading their way. He didn't have the heart to point them out. Not now. Not until he was certain they were being followed.

SIX

Annalise dozed off.

At least, she thought she had.

One minute, she was holding her hands toward the warmth streaming from the vent. The next, she was sitting in a cold car, staring at a windshield splattered with icy rain.

"What happened?" she muttered, expecting Mac to answer.

Only Mac was gone, the driver's seat empty.

Her heart jumped to her throat, and she sat up straighter, looking ahead, behind, to either side of the car. Trees. Trees. More trees. All of them glistening with a thick sheen of ice.

She glanced at her watch, but the numbers meant nothing. It was nearly midnight, but she had no idea when they'd left the used car dealership or how long she had been sitting in the car alone. She had no idea how long Mac had been gone, but she doubted it had been long. She couldn't believe he had left her alone at all!

Unless something had forced him to.

She didn't know where Mac had gone, but there was no way he had left her alone without a good reason.

She couldn't shake the feeling that something terrible had happened. Maybe Mac had pulled off the road because they were being followed and then gone to confront whoever was in the vehicle behind them. Worse, maybe he had used himself as a decoy to lead danger away from her.

Thinking about that, about Mac facing potential assassins to keep her safe, bothered her. She had always tried to take care of her problems, to not burden other people with her worries and fears. She had known, from spending time with her mother, from watching the way her illness affected friendships and romances, that most people wanted to be around for the good times and not for the bad ones.

Her marriage had proven that.

Gabe had told her he had turned to other women because she had been too clingy, too needy, too anxious and overwrought about building her career, having children and maintaining their relationship. He had felt overwhelmed by her needs, and he had wanted to be with someone who didn't hold on so tightly.

She hadn't believed him.

Not then.

She had called it what it was: the deepest kind of betrayal.

And she had called him what she had seen him as—a self-absorbed liar and cheat.

Years later, though, she had realized there may have been something to what he had said. She had always craved stability. She had wanted the neat, tidy home with the neat, tidy love. She hadn't wanted messiness. She hadn't wanted the highs and lows that had filled her childhood. Maybe she had been so desperate for that, she *had* clung too hard, tried too much to make their marriage perfect.

Since her divorce, she had tried even harder to be independent and to rely on herself. Now, she had no choice but to rely on Mac. He had the ability to keep her safe. He had proven that. But, she didn't want him to sacrifice his life to do it. Thinking about him out in the icy weather, facing off against men with guns who wouldn't hesitate to shoot filled her with dread. If he was in trouble, she couldn't just sit in the car and hope for the best. She had to do something to help.

She opened the door, shivering as it knocked against ice-coated pine boughs and sent cold drops of water into the car and onto her head. The world was a winter wonderland, the woods white-coated and shimmering. It reminded her of Christmas cards her mother would buy and hang from the fireplace mantel in their threadbare living room. They'd shared a tiny apartment in a not-so-nice section of Boston. The building had once been a huge Victorian home that had housed a large family, servants and staff. Their apartment had been a walled-in section of the third-floor attic area. Most of it had once been the maid's quarters. Aside from the tiny bedroom she had shared with her mother, there wasn't much to the place. A living room with a fireplace. A small kitchen and just enough room for a two-person table and chairs. A bathroom that had been carved out of a closet and had such a tiny shower, water had always sprayed the entire room.

Sometimes, Annalise missed it. The smell of furniture polish that her mother had used to try to improve the look of their ancient coffee table. The scent of bleach that was used to scrub the subway tiles in the bathroom. Her mother's cheap perfume.

She missed her mother.

They'd had plenty of good times mixed with the bad. Plenty of highs mixed with the lows. It hadn't always been easy, but they had made it work. If she were here, Annalise's mother would be out of the car and eager to help. Despite her mental illness, she had been strong and determined, intelligent and kind. Annalise wanted to be nothing less than those things. She wasn't going to cower in safety while someone was in danger.

She surveyed the area, trying to figure out how the car had gotten into the woods and where Mac had headed after he had parked it. She didn't see a road. No sign of the highway they'd been on when she'd fallen asleep. There were no footprints visible in the ice that coated the ground. He hadn't just disappeared. Something had made him leave the vehicle here, and something had forced him to abandon it and her.

No. Not her.

She didn't believe he would do that.

Not by choice.

The temperature had plummeted, icy rain turning to soft white flurries. She circled the car, making sure to keep it in sight as she tried to find a path or a road or some sign that Mac had been there. Nothing. It was as if he had been a figment of her imagination, as if he had never existed except in her dreams.

She knew that wasn't possible.

She hadn't imagined the race through the woods with him, the mine collapse, the sheriff's office. She certainly wasn't imagining the SUV parked under the boughs of a pine tree.

Where had he gone?

She didn't dare call out. She was too afraid of who might hear. They were being hunted by assassins and searched for by the sheriff. If she was found before she found Mac, would he survive? Would she?

She frowned, widening the circle she was making around the car, scouring the ground and the trees, searching for footprints, broken branches, anything that would give her a hint as to where he had gone.

When she finally spotted both, her heart jumped. All she had to do was follow the trail to him. It sounded easy enough, but she had a feeling it wouldn't be. Snow continued to fall, filling in footprints and she moved through the trees. If she wasn't careful, she would lose the trail and forget the way back to the SUV. Her stomach churned at the thought. It was cold. She wasn't dressed for the weather. It would be easy to die out in the wilderness. She couldn't wait at the SUV and hope for the best. She could freeze in the vehicle just as easily as she could freeze outside.

But, the pit in her gut was saying that she should have waited.

Leaving shelter and wandering through unknown territory, hoping to find Mac? Probably not the best idea she'd ever had. Wasn't it best to hug a tree? Stay in one place? Wait to be found?

She stopped, allowing herself to stand still, soft flakes of snow drifting through the tree canopy and settling on Mac's jacket. She turned a slow circle, looking for signs of civilization. There were no lights. No cleared land that she could see.

How deep was she in the forest?

How far from the road?

Her toes were already frozen, her feet like lead blocks attached to her ankles. Returning to the car might be the better option.

"What would Mac do? Keep going forward? Head back to the vehicle?"

"He wouldn't have left the vehicle in the first place," he said, his voice so surprising she screamed and jumped back, bumping into a tree and causing icicles to shower down from its branches.

"Where did you come from?" she demanded, whirling to face him.

His shoulders were coated with snowflakes, his hair covered with a layer of ice.

He was scowling at her through the darkness, his eyes flashing with irritation.

But to her, he looked like Christmas morning and birthday surprises all rolled into a six-foot-four package of joy.

"The cabin. I wanted to make sure the area was clear before we walked there together," he replied, still scowling. "I would have left you a note, but I didn't have anything to write with. If I'd known you were going to wake up and wander around on your own, I would have woken you up and had you come with me."

"I should have stayed with the vehicle. I was…"

"What?"

"Worried about you. It seems silly now. You're plenty capable of taking care of yourself, but I thought maybe you'd gotten into trouble or were trying to lead Moreno's thugs away from me."

"And, you thought you'd come save the day?"

"Something like that," she admitted. "Like I said, it seems silly now."

"Not silly. But, it's dangerous to leave the vehicle when it's this cold out. Especially out in the woods. It's easy to get lost on a night like to night."

"I realized that right before you found me."

"Come on. The cabin isn't far."

He hooked an arm around her waist and tugged her into his side. She fit well there, her arm just under his shoulder, her hand finding its way around his back. If she'd wanted to, she could have leaned her head against his shoulder, but, of course, she didn't. They were on the run from people who wanted her dead. They were hiding from the sheriff until they knew whose side he was on. They were in the middle of snow-shrouded trees, walking on ice-covered ground, shivering. This was not the time to be thinking about Mac as anything other than what he was: a guy who had gotten involved in her troubles and was stuck with her until they could find a way out of them.

Silence stretched between them, the quiet rustle of frozen foliage and muted thump of their feet the only sounds. It could have been any other night, and they could have been any other people walking through a snow-shrouded wood together. And, if they had been, if they weren't on the run, would she feel differently about Mac? Would she still want to move closer, or would she want to step away?

After her divorce, she'd had no interest in dating or relationships. She hadn't wanted to be hurt again. She hadn't wanted to be disappointed. She had told herself there was no room in her life for romance or dating, and she had believed it.

Did she still?

"You doing okay?" he asked.

"Probably better than you. I haven't been outside as long."

"I'm good. I'm used to working outside in all kinds of weather."

"What's going to happen at the ranch if you're not back in the morning?"

"I won't be, and the ranch will be fine. I've got a great manager and a good crew. Things will run smoothly until I return."

"I hope so. I'd feel terrible if it didn't."

"Why? You didn't cause this. You're just a victim of it."

"And, you have no reason to be a part of it."

"I was paid to keep you on the ranch and keep you safe. This is part of that."

The woods were thick, tall pine trees mixed with broad-trunked cedar and elm. A winter cocoon housing slumbering animals and wandering nocturnal creatures, the forest was a fantasy of ice, snow and greenery. For the first time since she had been pulled off the trail and attacked, she felt distanced from the threat, safe from the men who were after her.

"I appreciate it, Mac, but you know I would understand if you stepped back and let me deal with things alone."

"And, you know I'm not going to do that."

"I guess I do," she said, her arm still wrapped around him. She could have moved. They were walking at an easy pace, squeezing between trees together and causing snow and ice to fall from the branches. It would have been easier to walk single-file, to march ahead without touching, but he was as comforting as a velvet blanket on a cold night.

"You don't sound convinced."

"If I weren't, I wouldn't have left the SUV to find you. I would have assumed you had abandoned me."

"I guess that would have been a reasonable assumption. Look. We're here." He made the announcement as if they had reached a destination. All she saw were more trees.

"Is it an underground cabin?" she asked.

"No. Just one the woods are trying to consume. I haven't been out here in years. Some of the undergrowth needs to be cut back."

"Right." She still didn't see anything.

"To the left. Behind the two slender evergreens."

"There are a million skinny evergr..." She saw it, the sharp edge of an exterior wall. The steepled roofline.

"I searched the perimeter. It's clear. For now."

"What's that mean?"

"Everyone in town knows my grandfather owned land out here. In the decade prior to his death, he didn't hunt or fish much, but that doesn't mean people have forgotten that he used to."

"So, our time here is limited?" she commented as they walked around the side of the A-frame cabin.

"There was never any chance that it wasn't. All we need is a few hours to sleep and to come up with a plan. If we get that, we'll be fine. We have the SUV. I can return to the ranch, get my ID, and we can be on the road by first light."

"Heading where?"

"That's what we need to figure out," he responded, reaching past her to open the door. It creaked inward like a prop in a horror movie, the interior dark as pitch.

Mac must have seen the anxiety in her face.

He smiled into her eyes, flashing dimples that she had noticed one too many times. "I've already been in. No bears. No raccoons."

"No men with guns."

"None of those, either. Come on. Let's get inside before we both freeze." He gave her a gentle nudge, and Annalise stepped over the threshold into darkness.

Mac moved through the cabin in the dark, reaching the far wall and the shelves that he had helped his grandfather install two decades ago. A small kerosene lamp had been there ever sense. A few candles. A metal waterproof box with matches. He found that, opened it and took out a striker and match. He found the kerosene lamp next. He knew his grandfather, and he knew it would be filled with fuel. Andrew Davis didn't believe in taking chances. He believed in thinking ahead and preparing for anything.

Mac didn't think he had been prepared for losing his wife of fifty-five years. Her illness, the cancer treatments, the long and painful journey to accepting that Ada wasn't going to get better had taken its toll, but Patrick had still maintained the orderly, well-prepared life he had always aspired to.

Mac held the lamp and struck the match, a ritual he had learned years ago when he'd camped with his parents and siblings. Back then, living in Texas had meant Houston life. Lots of people and activity spread across flat land and golden fields. He had never imagined living on Sweet Valley Ranch. He had never once considered becoming a cattle rancher.

He struck the match and lit the wick, adjusting the flow of fuel so that the flame danced happily. The cabin was exactly the way Mac remembered. One room with a loft. A wood-burning stove the only source of heat, the ventilation system butting up through the crosshatched ceiling. There were several windows boarded up the day his grandfather had walked away for the last time. Not because Patrick hadn't planned to return, but because he had wanted to keep men and animals out while he was gone.

That was to Mac and Anna's advantage. With the windows boarded up, it would be impossible for searchers to see light through the woods. He set the lamp on the small coffee table that stood beside an old plaid sofa. His grandfather had taken it from the ranch when Ada had upgraded to leather. Mac had no idea how long ago that had been, but the plaid sofa had been in the cabin for as long as he could remember.

"This is cute," Anna said, her voice echoing in the quietness of the moment. A million memories were etched into four walls and three windows.

"My grandfather and grandmother use to stay here when they hunted and fished. That was before they had five kids."

"Five children? That's a large family."

"Not for a rancher. I think they hoped one of their kids would take over running the cattle business, but none of them were interested."

"That must have been disappointing," she said, walking to one of the shelves and lifting an old water pitcher.

"I don't think they felt that. My uncle Brady is a doctor. I have two aunts who are nurses. Uncle Mitchel is an accountant with a firm that handles investments for high-profile clients. My father is a computer engineer."

"Wow. That's a lot of achievement."

"It is, but my grandparents would have been proud of their kids regardless of what jobs they had. Once they started having children, my grandfather used the cabin.

My grandmother stayed home. Eventually, grandchildren were brought here for fishing weekends. There's a river a few miles away. Nice hunting, too. If you're into that."

"You're not."

"I prefer to not look through the scope of a rifle unless I have to. I buy my meat from the grocery store, and I'm happy with things that way," he replied. He had seen too much carnage during his time as a navy SEAL. He had no desire to see more.

"Were you in the military?" she asked, somehow guessing the truth he rarely shared.

"Yes."

"That's a hard job, Mac. And I'm sure you've seen a lot of things you'd rather not remember."

"You're right, but it's not something I talk about, so how about we focus on you."

She frowned. Her eyes were deep green-blue in the lamplight, her face glowing gold as the flames flickered and cast shadows through the room. "Focus on me?"

"On a coming up with a plan to figure out who leaked information about your whereabouts."

"Okay. Mind if I sit down while we do it? I'm beat."

"Go ahead." He motioned to a chair, then walked to a trunk that stood at the end of a queen-sized bed. There were blankets inside. Not the soft ones he had at the ranch. These were thick wool and made for keeping people warm.

He pulled one out and threw it over her shoulders, tucking the ends in around her neck. "Warmer?" he asked.

"Yes, but what about you?"

"There are plenty of blankets. And I'm not cold. This is the kind of weather I grew up with. I'm used to it."

"I grew up in Boston. It's even colder there."

"But how much time do you spend outside in it?"

"Plenty." She frowned. "Some. Okay. Not much. I walk from a parking garage to my office. From my apartment to my car. And, I run. But that keeps me warm."

"I have noticed you've got a fondness for running," he said, taking the second chair. They were close enough that their knees touched, but he didn't scoot back. Neither did she. Maybe they both needed a little closeness after their brush with danger.

"My mother got me hooked on it when I was a kid."

"She was a runner?"

"She was on medication that prevented her from being able to drive. We walked everywhere until I got old enough to keep up. Then, we ran."

"I'd ask what medication, but that would probably be overstepping," he said, curious despite himself. He hadn't asked much when Daniel presented the job opportunity. His grandfather had mortgaged the ranch to help pay for Ada's cancer treatment. Ranching wasn't as lucrative as it had once been, and he had been having trouble making the payments. It had come to a point where they were in danger of losing the ranch.

That's when Mac stepped in.

He had been home from Afghanistan, recovering from injuries. The ranch had seemed like the perfect place to recover, to regain some balance in his chaotic stressful life, to heal his body and his soul. He'd had no idea his grandfather was in financial trouble, but he'd seen the letters on the old roll-front desk. Warnings that the property would soon go into foreclosure. He'd emptied his account to pay the arears.

"You're welcome to ask. Nearly dying together must mean we have some kind of unbreakable bond, don't you think?" she asked with a wry smile.

"That's the way it works in the military," he replied, and her smile broadened. She was lovely in a wholesome girl-next-door way. Nothing overtly sensuous about her. She almost never wore makeup. Her hair was usually pulled back. She wore clothes that fit but that didn't contour every curve of her body.

Somehow, though, she drew the attention of every man on the ranch. More than one of the ranch hands had asked her out. He'd heard stories of her kind rejections, her pats on the back for the men who had dared try to get close. There had been murmurs about her having a boyfriend or fiancé somewhere. If she did, they hadn't seen one another in seven long months.

"That's what I've heard. So, we're buddies, now, huh? Comrades?"

"If you want," he replied, smiling despite himself, despite the circumstances, despite the danger they were still in.

"My mother had bipolar disorder," she said abruptly. "She was a great lady who just happened to have an illness. Her symptoms were mostly controlled by medication, but sometimes they weren't, or we didn't have money for what she needed, or she forgot to take the drugs." She shrugged as if it weren't painful to talk about, as if none of what had happened during her childhood mattered. "We ran because Mom sometimes thought we were being chased. As I grew up and matured, I began to recognize that as a sign that she wasn't taking her medicine."

"I'm sorry," he said, the words lame and useless but almost necessary to say.

"Why? I had a good childhood. Better than a lot of people's, anyway. Now, how about we discuss our next move before I fall asleep where I'm sitting?"

She wanted to change the subject.

That was obvious.

He would have preferred to keep chasing the rabbit down the hole. He'd been curious about Anna since the day he'd conducted the phony interview and hired her for the position of assistant cook. But she was right in saying they needed to stay focused. They had to come up with a plan. One that would get them the answers they needed.

Someone had leaked information to Archie Moreno.

Until they found out who, Anna's life would remain in jeopardy.

"Okay. Let's discuss it. Have you contacted anyone from your old life since you arrived in Texas?"

"Of course not."

"Have you seen anyone you recognize? Maybe a guest on the ranch? Someone who wouldn't normally be in Texas?"

"No. If I had, I would have let Marshal Avery know about it."

"Daniel Avery is the person who hired me. He said your whereabouts were on a need-to-know basis, and only a few people need to know."

She nodded, her ponytail sliding across her shoulder, pale against dark gray wool. "He told me the same. I have the contact number for someone who works for Justice Department. I've never had to call it, but Marshal Avery told me that if I did,

I'd be out of here faster than I could blink my eyes."

"So there are two people who knew where you were. Daniel and your emergency contact."

"The local sheriff's office, too. They were supposed to be informed."

"Daniel told you that?"

"Yes. He said that if things went south, he wanted to have local law enforcement on our side."

"Did he mention anyone else?" Mac stood and opened a drawer in the scuffed and dinged dresser that stood against a wall. There were dozens of pencils and small notebooks that had scribbled notes from scratched out games of tic-tac-toe. He grabbed one and turned to the first blank page. Jotting down Daniel's name as one means of the leak made him physically ill. He wrote River's name next. Then *mystery contact*. He didn't think anyone on the ranch knew that he was helping the Justice Department. He had certainly never mentioned it. Not even to his foreman, Lucas Sanders, a man he trusted with his life.

"Anyone else?" he asked, glancing at Anna.

She had her head on the table, the blanket pulled up around her head so that only her profile was visible. Her eyes were closed, lamplight and shadows flickering across smooth skin. He didn't wake her. They had a little time, and he wanted to think through their options before he presented them to her.

He pulled a second blanket from the trunk and wrapped it around her shoulders. The cabin was colder than he'd have liked, and he couldn't start the wood stove without sending up a smoke signal that announced their whereabouts.

Anna didn't move. Just like in the SUV, she seemed completely out. He grabbed the notebook and pen and sat opposite of her. Doing what he always did when he had a problem to solve, he jotted down names, dates, ideas. He added to his list of potential leaks. Anyone in the sheriff's department who might have known that there was witness hiding on the ranch. Any of the Mac's employees. From what he'd heard from Daniel, Archie Moreno had eyes and ears all over the country. If he wanted to find someone, it wasn't a stretch to believe that he could do it. Even while he was locked up in jail.

He also had money, and money was a powerful motivator.

Most people in Briarwood were content with their lives. There wasn't much poverty. People worked in the next town over—a forty-minute drive to big box stores, hospitals, restaurants. Or, they worked locally, serving meals at the diner or owning small businesses, or eking out livings on small farms and ranches. As far as he was aware, there wasn't an underworld of crime in the small town. It was what it appeared to be. An oasis from the hectic pace of modern life. A town where everyone seemed to know the business of everyone else, where neighbor helped neighbor and deep bonds were formed of decades and generations.

But that didn't mean it was perfect.

Crimes occurred. Men and women struggled. Life sapped people of their joy and purpose. It was possible someone in town was desperate enough to report back to Archie. It wasn't like Anna had stayed on the ranch. She had lived her life the way most people in Witness Protection did, moving through her new life as if it had always been hers. If she was telling the truth, if she had not contacted anyone from her old life, Mac needed to look closer to home.

Or closer to the Justice Department.

He needed to find out who he could trust and who he couldn't. Once Anna woke up, they'd go back to the SUV and head to Pine Gap. The forty minute drive to the larger, more metropolitan town would give him an opportunity to ask more questions, to dig a little deeper and make sure Anna was being honest about what she had done or not done.

Maybe she had followed all the rules.

Maybe she hadn't.

He would find out. Then he'd buy a burner phone and start making some calls. Someone, somewhere was fist-deep in Moreno's pockets. There were ways to discover who that was. Bank records. Phone records. Mac might not be in law enforcement, but he had plenty of military buddies who were or had been. One of them owned a private security company in Dallas. Mac thought Seamus Murphy would be just the person to help find the answers.

SEVEN

She dreamed about the courthouse. Walking out into the well-lit night, thinking about the weekend ahead and how she would fill her time. Not paying enough attention to the car that was rounding the corner until it was too late. The first shot fired, and a police officer fell back, his body armor keeping him from certain death as the bullet plowed into his chest.

Everything seemed to happen in slow motion.

She was on the ground, bullets pinging the cement stairs. A woman screamed in a voice she didn't recognize as her own.

She woke abruptly, her heart racing, her throat raw, her head pressed to Mac's chest, his hand stroking her hair.

"It's okay," he murmured. "You're all right."

Disoriented, unsure, she listened to his heartbeat and the soothing sound of his voice. For the first time in longer than she could remember, she felt completely safe and completely at home. As if everything that had come before had been wrong, and this one thing was absolutely right.

Only it couldn't be, because she was in MacArthur Davis's arms, in a cabin in the woods, being hunted by the police and by hit men.

She pulled back, nearly jumping to her feet, her heart still racing frantically.

"Slow down, Anna. Before you fall over." He cupped her elbow as she caught her balance.

"What happened?" she managed to say, her words as wobbly as her legs.

"You were screaming in your sleep," he replied, his tone one she'd heard him use with young children who visited the ranch with their parents and were sometimes afraid of the horses and cattle. Soothing. Soft.

"I'm not a child," she said, embarrassed that he'd heard her scream, that she'd woken in his arms, that she wished she were still there.

"I don't recall saying you were."

"You're speaking to me like I am."

"I'm speaking to you like I'd speak to a friend who had a nightmare and woke up screaming," he responded easily. Apparently not at all put off by her prickly tone. A tone he didn't deserve. One that embarrassed her more than all the other things combined.

"I'm sorry. You're were trying to help, and I shouldn't be snapping at you. It's just embarrassing to wake up screaming in a stranger's arms."

"I'm not a stranger, and why should you be embarrassed? You can't help the nightmares that are living in your head."

"Wouldn't you be? Waking up with your throat raw and your heart pounding, with someone you barely know right next to you?"

"Maybe the first time. After a while, you get used to it."

"That's easy to say when you're not the one who was screaming."

"It's not easy to say. I've lived it. I know how you feel," he responded easily. "So, how about we move on and forget it happened."

"Just like that?" she asked, wondering what he woke up screaming from. What memories haunted his mind and woke him in the middle of the night?

"How else would it be?" He smiled and lifted a small notebook from the table. "While you were sleeping, I came up with a list of possible leaks. If what you said about not contacting anyone from your old life is true."

"It is."

"Then the leak is someone in the Justice Department, someone on the ranch or someone you rubbed shoulders with in Briarwood."

"That's a whole lot of people, Mac."

"Who have you been closest to at the ranch?" he asked, opening the door and staring into a dusty white world.

"Stacey Hamlin." The head cook had taken Anna under her wing and helped her get acclimated to the kitchen and the job.

"I have her on my list. Anyone else?"

"Not really. Lucas drives the van to church every Sunday. I've talked to him, but not often enough to really call him a friend." The middle-aged foreman had always been kind, his dark eyes and easy smile putting Anna at ease. He had a wife and a couple of kids, and his family was usually what they talked about. She hadn't shared much about her life. It was easier to be quiet than to give details of the fake background she had been provided.

She had it memorized, of course, but it wasn't her real life, and she hated to lie to anyone. Especially people she liked.

"I have Lucas on the list, too," he responded, his tone grim.

"You don't sound happy about it."

"He's been working on the ranch longer than I've been here. He was my grandfather's foreman for ten years before I showed up and took over."

"Then why put him on the list?"

"Because he has access to places other people don't. My office. The safe where I keep bank records. My computer."

"Is there something he could have found that would have given my identity away?"

"No, but it's possible someone from Moreno's crime family reached out to a vulnerable member of my ranch family."

Family? She liked the way that sounded. As if they were more than just employees to him. "In that case, it could be anyone."

"It had to be someone who could get the key to your cabin. Remember the tracking device in your pedometer?"

She hadn't until he mentioned it. "I do keep the door locked."

She was careful about that. Almost obsessive, locking it and then checking it twice before she left.

"There are only three people on the ranch who have access to my office and the master set of keys. Stacey, Lucas, and my housekeeper, Lou. She is only in twice a week, and I'm usually in the office, but that doesn't mean she didn't get her hands on the key."

"You have security cameras at the ranch. Can we access them remotely?"

"Unfortunately, no. I have a friend in Dallas I'm going to contact. I want him to do a little research for me and maybe be a second set of eyes."

"Second set of eyes?"

"We have to go back to the ranch. I have cameras installed outside all the guest cabins. The security footage should show us who entered your cabin and planted the tracking device. With a little added manpower, we should be safe doing that."

"Manpower?"

"My friend is a security specialist. He knows how to keep clients safe."

"A bodyguard."

"I don't think he would want to be called that, but he knows how to secure locations, and he knows how to keep high-profile clients out of the line of fire. Between the two of us, we shouldn't have any trouble getting onto the ranch. Once we're there, we can access the footage and, hopefully, find out who placed that tracking device."

"And that will be an end to this nightmare?"

"It'll be the beginning of the end. We'll still need to prove a connection to Moreno, and we'll still need to be on guard against another attack. Moreno isn't going to give up if his first plan fails. He'll find someone else willing to do the job for him."

"Money talks," she murmured, crossing the room and joining him near the door. Sporadic flurries had turned to heavy snow, the flakes drifting listlessly from the cloudy sky. "What are you looking at? The snow?"

"Lights," he responded, the words like ice water in her veins.

"Flashlights?"

"Headlights. The road is that way." He gestured straight ahead. "See it?"

"All I see are trees."

"Stand here." He cupped her shoulders, maneuvering her so that she stood directly in front of him. She couldn't help remembering the way it had felt to be in his arms. How right and good and comfortable it had seemed. Heat seeped up her throat and into her cheeks, and she was glad the darkness hid the blush on her cheeks and the warmth of her face.

"See it now?" he asked.

She blinked, trying to focus on what he was saying and what he was trying to show her. In the distance, tiny lights hovered above the tree line. "It looks like fireflies, but I know it can't be."

"There's a deep ravine between us and

those lights. About a half mile of wooded area and a dirt road that is mostly over-grown. The paved road those cars are on isn't much to talk about, either. It's a wind-ing rural road that twists through the hills. Only people who live out here, hunt here or fish in the river use it."

"So, those lights shouldn't be there?"

"Maybe. It's possible a local had a flat or that someone's car broke down."

"But, you don't think that's the case."

"I don't. I think there's more than one car. I think it's probably the sheriff and a couple of his deputies. And I think if we don't get out of here soon, they'll be com-ing through the woods after us."

"Then why are we standing here discuss-ing it?"

"I've known River for most of my life. I don't want to believe he has anything to do with Moreno."

"So, you want to wait and see what he has to say?"

"My plan was to drive to the next town

over, buy a burner phone and call someone who can help us get phone records and bank records for anyone who had access to you."

"Has that changed?"

"I can't risk your well-being to go after answers I might not even get."

"There's risk either way. You said yourself that knowing someone doesn't make them innocent. It's possible the sheriff is involved. Even if he's not, he could have led the hit men to our location. There were deputies driving through town when we left. If a group of law enforcement officers left Briarwood, don't you think that would be like a red flag waved in front of a bull?"

"Your safety is my top priority, and there is safety in numbers."

"There is also safety in keeping a low profile and slipping under the radar, so let's go with the first plan," she urged. The last thing she wanted was to make more people Moreno's targets. His hired thugs wouldn't hesitate to kill anyone and everyone who stood in the way of her death.

She shuddered, pacing back to the table and grabbing one of the wool blankets that lay on the floor there. She slid out of Mac's coat and wrapped herself in the blanket.

"Let's go," she said, handing him the coat. "Unless you think we can't get out in the SUV without being spotted."

"I came in a back way that most people don't know about. It's three miles of rough road, but the SUV did fine." He was still staring at the light as if willing it to disappear or to move.

"What are you thinking?" she asked quietly, afraid her voice would carry through the quiet winter air.

"That there may be an army of people moving toward us, and we wouldn't know it until they were on us."

"I don't like the sound of that," she murmured, grabbing his hand. "Let's go."

"Hold on." He opened a small closet that stood near the rustic kitchen, rifled through clothes that hung from hangers and handed her a heavy parka. "Put this on. It'll be a lot easier than dragging a blanket through the woods."

She slid into it, watching as he pulled a lockbox from the back of a closet shelf. "Ammunition?" she whispered.

"Money. My grandfather believed in being prepared." He tucked the box under his arm, doused the kerosene lamp. "Let's go."

He walked outside, and she followed, certain there was a gleaming bull's-eye on her chest, begging for a bullet to be fired at it. Mac had been right. The trees were tall, dark shadows in a white landscape. Anyone could be hiding behind one of them. The sheriff. Deputies. Hit men. A friend who was really an enemy. She didn't want to believe anyone on the ranch had betrayed her. She didn't want to believe that her life was worth whatever small amount of money had been offered to give away her location.

But Mac's list was in her head. The names of people she had come to care about. People who she had thought cared about her. She couldn't shake the feeling that the betrayal of the past was repeating itself and that she had once again trusted someone she shouldn't have.

Snow blanketed the ground in a thin layer of white that would make tracking them easy. Mac tried to stay close to the thicker evergreens where the tree canopy prevented all but a few flakes from drifting into the woods. That made the trek back to the SUV more difficult. He watched every step, measured every movement, weighed it all in his mind before deciding whether to proceed. He had hoped to stay at the cabin until dawn. Anna was exhausted, and even he needed to sleep. But someone knew they were in the area. He didn't believe that the lights he'd seen were from random travelers who had run out of gas or gotten a flat tire. Either River had decided to check out the cabin they had stayed in when they were teens wanting to get away from town for a while, or someone who knew about the cabin had told Moreno's men that it might be a good place to check. Either way, he and Anna couldn't stay.

Neither of them spoke. The reality of the situation and the danger they were in were obvious. They didn't need to talk about it. They didn't need to discuss plans. They needed to move as quickly and quietly as they could.

He glanced over his shoulder, scanning the winter-gray world for signs they were being followed. The trees stood dark against the light landscape, their branches reaching toward the slate sky. Snow was still falling, the late winter storm not unusual for the area. The roads would be slippery with slush, and he would have to take his time. The last thing he wanted was to slide the SUV into a ditch. They'd be trapped. Sitting ducks waiting to be picked off by the first predator to arrive.

He did have his gun.

He also had whatever money his grandfather had left in the cabin. It had been a decade since he had seen what was in the lockbox. It was possible it was empty, but he hoped not. He had his wallet but using a credit or debit card was out of the question. He didn't want to be found because of a credit card transaction.

He didn't want to be found at all.

Not until he knew who the leak was.

He didn't want to believe he'd been betrayed by someone close, but the more he thought about the tracking device in Anna's shoe, the more concerned he became that someone who worked for him was also working for Moreno. The employee schedule was posted in the kitchen every Sunday. Even if it hadn't been, Anna was a creature of habit. She rose at the same time every day. She swept the front porch of her cabin every morning and evening. She walked out to the kitchen and mess hall a half hour before she was scheduled to work and always had a cup of coffee with Stacey Hamlin. After work, no matter the weather, she returned to her cabin, put on her running clothes and ran. Sometimes for an hour. Sometimes longer.

Anyone who worked on the ranch would know that.

Anyone who had spent even a few days watching Anna would know when she was going to be in the cabin and when she wasn't.

They reached the SUV, and he opened the passenger door, scanning the silent forest as Anna slid in. It was too quiet. Even on wintery nights, the woods were alive with nocturnal animals. Raccoons. Foxes. Coyotes. Deer. They roamed the hills, scavenging for food. Wild boars and large cats were also known to wander the woods at night. He had seen cougars, panthers and bobcats. He'd hunted with his grandfather and father when the population of wild boars had threatened the cattle that grazed just below the shadowed forest. Even on snowy nights, it shouldn't be this quiet and still.

The hair on his nape stood on end as he climbed in and started the engine. The road was just behind them, twin divots cut into a nearly impassable trail. The SUV bounced over ruts as he backed onto overgrown gravel and dirt.

"You're quiet," Anna said as he maneuvered through the darkness. He didn't dare turn on the headlights. The engine was enough of a beacon, calling anyone in the forest to investigate.

"Thinking."

"About?"

"The fact that someone planted a tracking device on your shoe."

"And?"

"It had to be someone who works for me. That doesn't make me happy."

"It could have been a visitor. It's not like you don't have dozens of strangers on your ranch every week," she pointed out.

"How many of them would know your

routine? Only someone who knew your schedule would have the guts to go in your cabin and plant that device."

"Some of the guests stay a week. That would be long enough to figure out when I work. Or to see me working and sneak to my cabin."

"Your cabin is on the opposite side of the ranch from the guest quarters."

"Still, if someone really wanted to, they could figure out where I was staying. It's not like I tried to hide it. I was behaving the way someone who had nothing to hide would. I wasn't trying to stay hidden or be surreptitious about my activities."

"I'd like to think you're right, but I have a feeling the traitor is a little closer to home."

"We need to get the security footage."

"First, we need to contact my friend in Dallas. If he can make the trip out here, we'll have another set of eyes and ears on the ground. Another protective shield between you and the people who are after you. Once that happens, we're heading back to the ranch."

"Are you going to let the sheriff know our plans?" she asked, shifting in her seat and staring out the back window. They were nearing the old paved road he'd driven down while she slept.

"I'll call him from the burner phone. After I call my friend."

"Do you think he's involved?"

"I hope not," he said. He didn't believe River could be bought for any price. From the time he was young, he'd had a high sense of justice. He'd skirted the law and gotten into trouble as a teen, but he'd never done anything to hurt another human being. His reputation for compassion and fairness had gotten him elected as the youngest sheriff in the Briarwood's history. He'd held that position for ten years without any real competition. Mac had considered him a good friend and a great guy. He still did.

But, anything was possible.

Experience had taught him that, and he wasn't going to take any chances.

"Look, Mac, I know you were paid to do a job. I get that you want to follow through and do what you agreed to, but there isn't enough money in the world worth your life. I was thinking that when I woke up in the SUV, and you weren't there. If something happened you because of me, I couldn't live with myself."

"If something happens to me, it won't be because of you. It will be because of Moreno and his hired thugs."

"I don't think you understand what I'm saying."

"I understand perfectly. You think that because there is a threat against me, I should toss you to the wolves and hope they're so busy tearing you apart they forget about me." The SUV bounced onto the paved road, a long empty stretch of ice, slush and snow unmarked by tire tracks.

"That isn't what I'm saying."

"Then, what are you saying?"

"You have an entire community of people relying on you to keep the ranch going. How many people work for you? Thirty? Forty?"

"Twenty-five full-time employees. Eighteen part-time."

"Right. And most of the full-time employees live on the ranch. Free of charge. Take Stacey for example."

"How about we don't?" he muttered. He knew what she was going to say. He understood her point. Most of the people who worked for him would have trouble finding a job somewhere else. They had been ranch hands or cooks or housekeepers for most of their lives, and there weren't many opportunities for that kind of work in Briarwood. They'd have to leave the community they loved and head to another town where housing wouldn't be free and meals weren't paid for.

He did right by his employees.

The same way his grandfather and great-grandfather had.

They were family, and if something happened to the ranch, if it went under, if he weren't around to run it, their lives would be irrevocably changed.

"She's saving for a house in town. There's a little ranch for sale, and she's been eyeing it. Her daughter just got divorced and is talking about moving back here, and Stacey would love to have a place for her and her granddaughter. If something happened to you, and her job was gone, that dream would never come true."

"She never mentioned that to me."

"Probably because you've never spent three hours peeling potatoes with her," Anna said absently, her gaze on the white-coated road and the distant lights of farmhouses that dotted the area. "If you let me out here, I can walk to one of those houses. You can go back to the ranch and call River and tell him that I ran off, and you don't know where I went."

"No."

"What do you mean, no?"

"Exactly what I said. No. I'm not letting you out. You aren't walking to a farmhouse. I'm not calling River."

"I don't see why not. I'm an adult, and I'm perfectly capable of getting myself out of this situation."

"First, River would never believe that I let you escape. Second, I'm not here because you're not capable. You are obviously an intelligent, strong, capable human being. I'm here because Moreno isn't going to stop until his crime family is shut down or until you're dead. I'm not willing to allow the second thing to happen."

"Mac—"

"The day you arrived at Sweet Valley Ranch, we became partners in our effort to put him away. Just because you didn't know it, didn't mean it wasn't true. I had all the facts going into this. I made the decision. I'm sticking to my end of the bargain. The partnership doesn't end until the trial is over and he is convicted and sentenced to a life behind bars. That's the way

I've seen it from the beginning. It's the way I still see it."

"I don't want anything to happen to you. I already have enough guilt. I can't live with more," she said so quietly he almost didn't hear.

He had done his research. He'd read newspaper accounts of what had happened in Boston. He'd watched news footage of the aftermath of the shooting that had left a prosecuting attorney and a federal witness dead, two police officers and a FBI defense attorney wounded. Annalise Rivers had been caught in the cross fire of a battle she had no part in. The two police officers had also survived, but neither had seen the shooter. Anna had.

She'd fisted her hands and was staring straight ahead, maybe still looking at the lights. Or, maybe, looking into the past, reliving the shooting.

He understood. He knew how quickly the past could rise up and take over. He had spent years working through symptoms of PTSD. He had spent countless hours in therapy learning to live with the guilt he'd had for surviving when people he had loved like brothers had not. He lifted one of her hands, smoothing his thumb over her knuckles. "What happened wasn't your fault," he said.

"I know."

"And you couldn't have prevented it." She shrugged.

"You couldn't have."

"I saw the car. If I'd realized what was going to happen, I could have warned the police. They could have stopped the shooter before he fired the first shot."

"You know that isn't true."

"No. I don't," she said so wearily, he wondered how many hours she had spent reliving those moments, imagining a different outcome, believing she could have changed things.

"Have you talked to anyone about this?"

"Who would I talk to? I gave up my friends, my job, my colleagues and my church family when I entered Witness Protection. I can't discuss it with anyone here, because no one is supposed to know about it."

"Did you tell Daniel you were struggling?"

"Marshal Avery? I don't have contact information for him. Even if I did, what would I say? It isn't like I'm not handling things."

"The nightmare you had says something different."

She tugged her hand away and didn't respond.

"It isn't something to be ashamed of. I had nightmares nearly every night for a while. I spent a lot of time in counseling dealing with that and a few other things that resulted from my military years," he said as he eased around a curve in the road. They'd reached one of the farmhouses that edged the road, the light from its front porch reflecting off a pristine white yard and a long driveway. No cars visible, but there were fresh tracks in the snow. Odd since all the lights in the house were off.

He tensed, pressing on the gas, giving the SUV a burst of speed as he rolled past. The road was slippery and hazardous, but several vehicles had left tracks in the layer of slush and snow.

"What's wrong?" Anna asked, her voice tight with concern.

"Your seat belt is on, right?"

"Yes."

"Good." He accelerated more, the SUV fishtailing as headlights appeared on the driveway and a car sped toward the road, sliding out behind them, high beams glaring in his rearview mirror. A dark car. A sedan. Front-wheel drive and unable to keep up in the icy conditions, it spun into a ditch, exhaust puffing into the dark sky. More headlights appeared, flashing on the road ahead of them.

Moreno's men had found them again.

Which only confirmed what Mac had already suspected. Someone close to him, who knew about the mountain cabin and the roads in and out of it, had betrayed him.

River?

One of the ranch hands?

Lucas?

He didn't know, but he planned to find out, and whoever it was would pay.

For now, Mac was sticking to his plan. Get to a town where he could buy a burner phone. Contact Seamus. Line up more manpower to help protect Anna and find the leak.

First, he had to outrun their tail.

He cut to the left, bouncing off the road and into a field he knew connected to the highway, picking up speed as the SUV's tires found traction on frozen dirt and foliage.

Lights flashed as a vehicle tried to follow them into the field. It bottomed out and got stuck in a small ditch.

Mac stayed focused. His hands on the steering wheel, his mind spinning through endless possibilities. Someone he cared about had betrayed his trust and his loyalty. Eventually, he would allow himself to hurt over it, to mourn.

For now, his one goal, his only goal, was to get Anna to safety.

EIGHT

Annalise had been through a lot in her life. She'd spent her childhood watching her mother be mistreated by men who had taken advantage of her kindness and her fragile mental state. She had spent her tween and teenage years helping run the home, making sure bills were paid, and doing everything she could to make certain her mother was okay. College had been years of working odd jobs and long hours, commuting back and forth to school because she didn't want to leave her mother. She knew her mother would be okay on her own, but the bond between them had been forged through years of taking a combined stand against the unfairness of the world and of life. She would have stayed home during law school if she could have, but it had been too far, and her mother had insisted she pursue her dreams.

If Anna had known the outcome of leaving, she wouldn't have gone. Just like if she had known Gabe was a lying, cheating hypocrite, she wouldn't have married him. She certainly would have changed the outcome the day of the shooting, if she had known that the car rounding the street corner contained an assassin.

Life had taught her that she had no control. She should have used that to fuel her determination to enjoy the moments she had, to live every day with joy and enthusiasm. She should have taken vacations and gone shopping with girlfriends instead of working on cases that she had already spent dozens of hours prepping for.

She should have bought the house in the country she and her mother had once dreamed of. The quiet property with the fenced yard and room for a dog and cat and chickens.

Instead, she had made sure her life was carefully structured. Predictable. Ordered. Organized. Mondays were for laundry. Tuesdays and Thursdays for working out at the gym. She ran five days a week. Six if she didn't have court on Monday morning. She paid her bills on the same day every month. She ate out once a week, got together with girlfriends after church on the third Sunday of every month.

And now, she was going to die in an icy field, far away from friends that she hadn't spent nearly enough time with. No family. No husband. No children. Not even a pet to mourn her passing.

She swallowed down grief that she had no business feeling.

She'd had a good life. A great one. Even with all the struggles and heartaches, she had always had blessings to be thankful for. If she had things she was sorry for, they were her own doing.

And, if she could go back, if she could change things, she would.

She gripped the dashboard as the SUV bounced across snow-covered grass, powered up a slippery hill and fishtailed onto the highway.

"Maybe you should slow down," she managed to say through gritted teeth.

"We lost them in the field. I want to put some distance between us and any patrol cars that might be heading this way," he responded, still accelerating, slush and ice flying onto the windshield.

"If we spin out and die, that will defeat the whole purpose of driving like a maniac in snowy conditions." The comment slipped out before she could stop it.

Mac didn't seem to take offense.

"I may not seem to be taking precautions, but I've driven in worse conditions in a vehicle a lot harder to control in icy weather."

"If that's supposed to make me feel better, it doesn't."

"I'm not going to do anything that would risk your life."

"Or yours?"

"You're my priority." He took a curve in the road, the SUV fishtailing again, headlights still off.

"Why?" she asked. She really wanted to know. Not some canned answer about accepting a job and having to follow it through to the end. Mac could have abandoned her at any time during the night, and she wouldn't have faulted him for it.

"Do me a favor. Open the lockbox. I want to see if my grandfather's stash of cash is still there." He was changing the subject, rattling off the combination so quickly she had to rush to grab the box from the seat and spin through the numbers.

As a distraction technique, it was effective.

For a few moments, all she was thinking about was getting the box open. Once the lock popped, she lifted the lid and stared into a box filled with money. "When you said a stash, I thought you were talking about a few dollars."

"Is it more than that?" He glanced at the box, his eye widening. "I guess we have enough for a burner phone."

"And a plane ticket back to Boston," she murmured. There were several hundred-dollar bills, a dozen fifties and enough twenties that she couldn't have carried them in her purse.

"Not yet," he said.

"What?"

"We're not going to Boston yet. If we can find the leak and get a firm connection with Moreno, the prosecutor will have an even better case, and you'll be that much safer until the trial. When is that? A couple weeks?"

"Are you trying to distract me?" she asked, counting the twenties and then carefully removing ten before closing and locking the box.

"Yes."

"At least you're honest about it."

"Why wouldn't I be?"

"People aren't always. Not when they want something."

"The only thing I want is to get off this highway before we're spotted," he replied as she reached over and tucked the money into his coat pocket.

"I'll leave the rest in here." She slid the box under the seat, trying not to focus on the road again. On the slush. The ice. The snow. According to the dashboard clock it was nearly four in the morning. The sun should rise in a few hours. The temperature would rise with it. The snow would turn to rain and traveling would be safer.

She shifted in her seat, looking out the back window. The road was empty. "I guess we lost them."

"For now. Someone who is working with them knows me well enough to know about the cabin and to know what road I would take to access. They were waiting for us."

"I'm sorry."

"For?"

"It isn't fun to be betrayed by someone you care about."

"No, it isn't. But, I'll deal with that after we contact my friend and figure out who leaked your whereabouts to Moreno."

"Do you think your friend will help us?"

"Yes. We were Navy buddies. We look out for each other."

"Like you and Marshal Avery?"

"Yes."

"It must be nice to have people you can count on like that." She faced forward again. A road sign announced the off-ramp that led to Pine Bluff.

"You don't?"

"If you don't slow down, you're going to miss the Pine Bluff exit," she pointed out, ignoring his question.

"Changing the subject?"

"Yes."

"I won't ask why. Until after this is over." She didn't ask what he meant.

"Pine Bluff?" she repeated. "The exit is right there."

"I think it's better to drive a while longer. Pine Bluff is the last decent-sized town between us and Abilene."

"Exactly. You'll be able to get a phone there and make your call."

"But we won't be able to stay there for any amount of time. Anyone who knows this area knows Pine Bluff. Moreno's henchmen have already seen the SUV. They know what I'm driving, and they'll be looking for it. I want to hole up somewhere until I can get backup that I trust."

"Your friend in Dallas?"

"Yes."

She frowned, biting her lip to keep from asking all the questions that were filling her head. She wanted to know how long they had served together. What they had done in the Navy. If they had been injured. When they had gotten out. She wanted to ask if they visited every year or just kept in contact via phone.

She wanted to ask about Mac's past.

His life in the military and his life as a child. His family. His goals.

That scared her.

Mac seemed like a good guy. She had never seen him lose his temper or mistreat someone. She had never heard him say a bad word to anyone, criticize harshly or demean a client or employee. He had a steady, even way of approaching life that made the people around him comfortable. He was obviously protective and dedicated to keeping his word.

But, that didn't mean she should be looking at him any differently than she did other men in her life. She certainly shouldn't be wondering about his past. She shouldn't be getting attached to the idea of getting to know him, of spending more time with him, of learning everything there was to know about his life.

But, she was, and she knew it.

And, that was a surefire way to be hurt again.

She frowned, pulling the borrowed coat

closer and settling deeper into the seat. She needed to return to Boston and her life. That was what she should be focused on. Anything else could only bring her trouble and heartache. Sure, she had been lonely sometimes. There had been nights when she had returned home after a fifteen-hour day and longed to have someone to talk to, but she had tried marriage. It hadn't worked out. She'd had roommates during law school. That had been fine, but she didn't want to clean up messes that weren't hers, fight for shower time or try to figure out laundry schedules. She wanted to share her heart, but she didn't want it broken again.

"Maybe a dog. They never lie to you, and they certainly don't cheat, and any messes they make are just because they're dogs. Not because they're slobs," she murmured.

"What's that?" Mac asked.

"I think I'll take a catnap while you're driving," she replied. She closed her eyes before he responded, leaning her head against the cold window and praying that the nightmare would be over soon and that she could return home to Boston and the safe, predictable life she had built there.

She wasn't sleeping.

The cadence of her breathing was too uneven, her body too tense, but Mac didn't bother asking why she was pretending. They both had troubles they were dealing with. They both had private struggles and secret pain. She had every right to keep her own counsel, to sink into herself and let the world fade away.

He exited the highway, merging onto the interstate. It was a straight shot to Abilene. A hundred miles of nothing but ranchland and farms, homesteads and a few small towns. Another two hundred miles from there to Dallas. He had made the trip a few times over the years, visiting Seamus and a few other buddies who had settled in the area. It had been a few years, though. The ranch took up all his time and energy. As much as he tried to keep up with the lives of his friends, he sometimes went months without checking in.

Seamus wouldn't hold that against him.

If he could, he would help.

If he couldn't, he would know who could. Unlike Mac, Seamus stayed in close contact with old friends. He had a network of people across the country who he had met and made friends with. His tough, hard-edged exterior belied a softer exterior. He would do anything for a friend. Even put his life on hold to help. In a fight, though, he was a formidable opponent. He fought hard, and he fought to win. He had been the guy everyone on their SEAL team had wanted as a flanker. The person who everyone trusted implicitly. He had been injured in the same IED explosion that had ended Mac's military career, but his face had still been the first one Mac had seen when he had come out of surgery.

The drive to Abilene took less than two hours, snow slowly turning to sleet and rain as Mac drove south and connected with Interstate 20. He expected to be pulled over by the state police, but traffic was sparse, police presence nil. Hopefully, River was focusing state and county attention on Pine Bluff, targeting resources in that direction.

It was still early, the sun just edging above the horizon as he pulled into a Walmart parking lot and parked the SUV close to the entrance. There were several vehicles parked nearby and a few eighteen-wheelers on the outskirts of the parking area.

"We made it," Anna said, straightening in her seat. "Let's go in and get the phone. I don't know about you, but I'm anxious to get back to my life."

She started opening the door.

He reached across her and held it closed, his forearm brushing her muscular thigh. She stilled, all the excitement and energy reined in as she stared into his eyes.

She was beautiful.

There was no question about that.

Large eyes. High cheekbones. Smooth skin with just a few freckles on her nose and cheeks. Fair hair that she usually pulled back from her face. A slim, muscular figure. Mac had spent years telling himself he was too busy to pay much attention to the women who came and went on the ranch. He had plenty of highbrow clients who were there for a good time, more than a few single women who had been actively looking for a partner. He had no time for games. Even if he did, he wouldn't have played them. For the past few years, he had accepted the bachelor life and been happy with it.

Now, he wondered if the reason he hadn't been noticing the women who came and went was because none of them had been the right woman.

Until Anna, there had been no one who drew his attention and kept it. Until her, he hadn't given any woman more than a passing glance.

"Sorry," he said, pulling back, his arm sliding across her thigh again. She blushed, the warmth in her cheeks obvious even in the dimly lit interior of the SUV.

"No need to apologize," she said brusquely. "We're both adults. I think we can handle a little unintentional touch. Now, how about we get moving?"

"I want you to stay here."

She'd grabbed the door handle again, but she didn't open the door. "Why?"

"Because River probably issued a BOLO for us. If not because he is involved, then because he is worried about us and wants to get us in custody before Moreno's men find us again. The police will be expecting a man and a woman together. If this were normal shopping hours, there would be dozens of couples walking in and out of the store. It's not. You stay here, ducked down so no one can see you. I'll go in. I'll be out as quickly as I can."

"I don't like that idea."

"Have you liked any of my ideas so far?"

he asked as he took the twenties she'd tucked into his coat pocket and put them in his wallet.

"I'm sure if I think long enough I can remember one that I was keen on," she replied. Her voice was light, a half smile on her lips, but he could see the concern in her eyes.

"It's going to be okay, but just in case something unexpected happens, I'll leave you the keys." He took them from the ignition and placed them in her hand, folding her fingers over them and squeezing gently. "I'm also going to give you my friend's business card. His name is Seamus Murphy. He owns a security company in Dallas. Tell him I gave you his contact information." He took the well-worn card from his wallet and set it on the dashboard.

"I would rather not have to do that," she said, her voice raspy and dry with fear. He didn't want to leave her in the SUV any more than she seemed to want to be left, but they were a lot more noticeable together than they were alone.

"You won't. Like I said, this is just in case something unexpected happens."

"Do you know how many times unexpected things have happened to me? Do you know how many times my life has been thrown into turmoil because of stuff that shouldn't have happened but did?" Her voice cracked, and she looked away. He wasn't sure if she was referring to the shooting in Boston or something else, but he didn't want to leave her defeated and uncertain.

He touched her chin, urging her to meet his eyes again. "Nothing unexpected is going to happen. No one knows we're here, and no one is going to know. Stay here. I'll be back as soon as I can." His finger trailed the curve of her jaw, skimming over silky flesh and soft strands of loose hair before he forced himself to turn away, to exit the vehicle, to walk toward the store as if he wanted to do it.

He was worried too.

He knew as well as she did that things could go wrong and often did. But he had to trust in his plan. He had to have faith that God was in it. He had to move forward with confidence and purpose. Hesitation could kill a man. He had seen that during his time overseas. Moving forward on any plan was better than sitting frozen with uncertainty.

He walked into the store and went straight to the electronics section. He didn't waste time. He knew what he was looking for. He bought three phones and paid cash, ignoring the cashier's curious look as he grabbed a few protein bars and packages of almonds onto the conveyor belt, adding several bottles of juice and water, and waited to be rung up. The cashier raised an eyebrow when Mac handed her twenties to pay. She checked one at a time, using a UV light to study each banknote. Finally satisfied, she bagged his purchases and handed him change.

Mac had the first phone ready for use as he walked out of the store, and he was dialing Seamus's number as he slid into the SUV.

"Murphy here. What's up?" Seamus said curtly.

Mac met Anna's eyes and gave her a thumbs-up.

"Hey, Shay, it's Mac."

"Is it now?" he asked, his Irish accent barely noticeable. He'd spent the first fifteen years of his life with his mother's family in Ireland. He'd never said much about the reasons why he had joined his father in the US, but Mac knew it wasn't a happy story or a good one. "Then why don't I recognize the number?"

"Because I'm in a bit of a…bind, and I can't use a traceable phone."

"You're at the ranch?" he asked, his voice sharp.

"No. I'm in Abilene."

"That's a little over two hours from here." He muttered something under his breath. "How much trouble? The kind that could get you arrested? Or the kind that could get you killed?"

"Both."

"In that case, it'll be best if you stay out of sight. I'll come to you. Where are you?"

"In a Walmart parking lot on the western side of the city."

"Not going to do you much good to sit there. The sun is going to be up in an hour. You'll be clear pickings for whoever is after you. Hold on. I'm looking at a map. There's a motel just off I-20. About seven miles east of your location. Looks like the kind of place a man can check in using cash. White House Inn is the name. Check in there. Call me with the room number. Other than that, no contact until I arrive. We'll figure things out when I get there." He disconnected, the silence the only indication that he was ending the call.

Mac tossed the phone onto the console and took the keys Anna was holding out to him.

"What now?" she asked, her skin pale, her eyes deeply shadowed. A couple of hours of sleep would do her good. He'd worry about rest for himself after Seamus arrived.

"We check into a motel until Shay arrives."

"How long will that be?"

"A couple of hours. He drives fast when he has somewhere to be." He pulled out of the parking lot and merged onto I-20. The city was beginning to wake, cars speeding along the road as people began commuting to work. He drove the speed limit, checking his rearview mirror as he spotted the White House Inn and exited the freeway. If they were being tailed, it wasn't obvious. He did a slow trek around the area, driving from the hotel to a nearby fast food restaurant and ordering two cups of coffee. Black for him. Two creams for Anna.

He handed her the cup as he pulled away. "There are almonds and protein bars in the bag. Go ahead and eat something."

She rifled through the bag and pulled out two protein bars, opening both. She took his coffee and placed it in the cup holder, then handed him a protein bar. "I'm not the only one who needs to eat."

"I ate dinner last night."

"I did…" Her voice trailed off. "Maybe I didn't."

"You didn't."

"How do you know? You weren't there."

"You never eat before you run."

She frowned. "That's true."

"You grab some fruit and protein when you're done and go to your cabin. I figured you ate there. Since you didn't make it back last night, you're probably hungry."

"Now, that you mention it, I am." She bit into the protein bar. "Do you think your friend will really be here in a couple of hours?"

"Yes."

"So, he'll just drop whatever he was doing and leave? No packed bags or getting ready? Just climb in a car and drive here?"

"Yes."

"Wow."

"Wow what?"

"That's the kind of friend we all wish we had, I guess."

"I'd do the same for him."

"Then you are also the kind of friend we all wish we had."

"Wouldn't you do what you could for a friend?" he asked, pulling into the White House Inn parking lot. The place had seen better days, the white paint gray with age, the windows smudged and cracked.

"Well, yes. But not everyone is like that." She shrugged, taking a sip of coffee and smiling. "That's good coffee."

"Or, you're really desperate for caffeine," he responded, returning her smile as she took another bite of protein bar. Color had returned to her cheeks, and she looked more energetic, her normal good humor replacing fatigue and fear.

"I was definitely desperate for caffeine. It's just the way I like it, by the way. How'd you know?"

"You have a cup of coffee every Sunday after church. Always with two creams."

"I do?"

"You also eat exactly half a glazed doughnut. You always give the other half to Stacey."

"That's probably true. I do like glazed doughnuts, but not enough to eat the whole thing." She frowned. "You've spent a lot of time studying what I do, Mac."

"You've spent six months on the ranch. You've attended church every Sunday. I didn't have to study you to notice those things. I just had to pay attention."

"Ha! Tell my ex that. We dated for four years and were married for three, and he still always brought me coffee with sugar and no cream." She pressed her lips together and turned her attention to the motel. "I guess we should see if they have a room."

"Seeing as how the parking lot is nearly empty, I'd say it's a good possibility they do." He wanted to ask more about her marriage and her ex, but it wasn't his business. He was there to keep her safe and to get her to trial, not to dig into her life and her past.

But he *was* curious.

He had been curious since the day she'd arrived at the ranch. He could admit that. What he couldn't do was allow himself to be distracted by it. He had to stay focused on the mission and the goal. He couldn't allow anything or anyone to get in the way of that.

Not even himself.

But looking into Anna's eyes, seeing the concern and fear in her face, he had a feeling that might be a bigger challenge than he imagined.

"Are we going to sit here staring at each other all day or go check into the motel?" she asked, turning away and opening the door.

He took several twenties from the lockbox before stepping out of the SUV and surveying the parking lot. He had pulled around to the back of the building, parking near bushes and the dumpster. They partially blocked the view of the street.

She climbed out before he had a clear visual of the surrounding area.

"Get back in the car," he said. "We don't know if we were followed."

"You spent most of the drive looking in the rearview mirror. If we were followed, you'd know it," she said confidently.

She was right and he wasn't going to waste time arguing about whether she was in the vehicle or out of it. He grabbed the lockbox and took her hand. She didn't resist as he crossed the parking lot and entered the back door.

They could have been any couple checking into a hotel after a long night driving. Their fingers entwined, their steps synced, they walked through a dingy hall and made their way to a small lobby. An elderly man sat in a leather chair behind a dusty counter, his hair sticking out in gray tufts around his thin face. He looked up from a book he was reading as they approached, his gaze jumping from Mac to Anna.

"Forty dollars a night. You pay the same amount whether you stay an hour or six weeks," he said gruffly, grabbing a key from a drawer in the desk.

Mac handed him two twenties.

"You paying by the night?" the man asked as he shoved the cash into another drawer. "Because if you're staying more than one, you gotta pay up front."

"Just one night," Mac responded.

"Room 105 is at the end of the hall." He gestured to the left. "Place is quiet. I like to keep it that way."

"No problem."

"No security cameras, and I don't talk. You pay your tab and keep quiet, I don't care why you're here." He thrust the key in Mac's direction and turned his attention back to the book.

"Thanks," Mac said, his hand tightening around Anna's as he walked through the narrow hall. It smelled of stale smoke and vomit, the carpet so threadbare, plywood was visible beneath it. Room 105 was the last door to the left, next to an emergency exit that Mac was happy to see. The more escape routes, the better.

He unlocked the door and pulled Anna into the room with him. They had been running for hours, and he wanted to stop, to think through plans and to make certain he had everything in place to do what needed to be done: head back to the ranch, find the person who had betrayed him, and stop him before he could do any more damage.

Anna's life depended on his ability to do that.

He wouldn't forget that. He couldn't forget it. He certainly wouldn't let his anger and hurt cloud his judgment. Once Seamus arrived, he'd discuss the plan with him. If Seamus agreed it was sound, they would move forward. If not, they would come up with a new one.

Whatever they decided, Anna's wellbeing had to be a priority. Not just because she was an assignment he had agreed to take, but because she was a person that he was beginning to care about. Someone he wanted to get to know better.

After this was over.

After they were safe.

After he made sure she could live the life she wanted. The one she had left behind in Boston.

He shoved the thought away.

He would worry about that later.

For now, he needed to focus on keeping them both out of the line of fire.

NINE

She'd been in worse places.

But not recently.

Anna paced the small room, skirting a rickety table and two small chairs, ignoring the coffee maker that sat on a stand near a window that looked out onto the parking lot. Mac had closed the curtains and turned on the lights, then left her in the room while he did what he called a perimeter check. She opened the door to the bathroom, glancing into the clean and sparse room. White tile. Two thin towels hanging from a rack. No soap or shampoo. She closed it again and crossed to another door. Like the door into the hall, it had an interior lock and a bolt. She pulled it open and found herself staring at another door.

She tried the knob. It was locked. She assumed it opened into another guest room. She closed the door, locked it and threw the bolt home.

She wanted to feel safe.

She didn't.

Despite what the front desk help had said, the motel seemed like the kind of place that had seen its share of criminal activity and police raids. If the police showed up and found her there, would they recognize her? She had no doubt River was looking for them, but would he have gone so far as to contact other counties? They weren't criminals. They'd had every right to leave the sheriff's department. She was familiar enough with the law to know that.

Mac seemed to think River would call in the county and state police for help. He knew the sheriff better than she did, and she had to assume he was correct. Which made being in the motel feel more like being a lone duck in the middle of a pond during hunting season than being a protected witness waiting to testify at a federal trial.

She frowned, making another quick circuit of the room.

Moreno played for keeps.

He had a multimillion-dollar business motivating him, and he wasn't going to give it up without a fight. He had proven that many times over. His adversaries died or they disappeared. People who stood in his way didn't stand there for long. He knew how to make things happen, and he knew how to keep his hands clean. He ran several high-end restaurants in Boston that served as a front for his illegal activities. At least, that is what law enforcement had suspected. Up until the courthouse shooting, they hadn't been able to prove it. Moreno was careful. He didn't make mistakes. If any of his associates did, they disappeared before it could affect him.

Now, one of his close associates, his hired gun, had made a colossal error, and it could ruin everything Moreno had built.

He wasn't going to accept that. He would make every effort to change it. That meant getting rid of the only witness who could link his hired hit man to the shooting. Annalise had been aware of that before she had entered Witness Protection. The likelihood of her death if she had stayed in Boston had been explained to her, and she had been given a choice. Stay and be under twenty-four-hour protection or go into hiding.

It hadn't been a real choice.

She had watched two men be gunned down while armed police officers stood inches away. She had known her safety depended on going into hiding and staying there. She had played by all the rules she had been given. She had done everything she had been told.

She had still been found.

She needed to call her emergency contact. She had to at least touch base with the Justice Department. If Marshal Avery got wind of her disappearance, he would send people out looking for her. She didn't want to be found. Not until she knew who had leaked her location to Moreno.

She frowned, crossing the room and checking the lock on the door. She was tempted to pull back the curtain and look outside. She wasn't sure what she thought she would see. The nearly empty parking lot? The city beyond, modern buildings jutting up across a flat landscape? A few hills capped with a hint of white from the storm that had blown through?

She certainly wasn't expecting to see one of Moreno's men slinking toward the motel. She didn't think she would see police officers either. Mac had been careful. She'd seen the way he'd watched the rearview mirror. She knew he hadn't taken chances.

It still seemed too good to be true that they had escaped.

Moreno was smart.

He was cunning.

And he didn't like to lose. He hired people who could get jobs done. Not people who messed up.

A rotary phone sat on the bedside table. She lifted the receiver, listening to the hum of the dial tone. She could make the call to her emergency contact, explain the situation, ask for an armed escort to Boston, but she had no idea who she could trust. That was hard. It was even harder to realize that there wasn't one person in Boston she was tempted to call. She had plenty of work associates she was certain she could trust but none of them were close friends. She didn't have numbers memorized. Even if she did, she wouldn't have called to unload all her bottled-up terror and anxiety. She couldn't have asked the FBI to step into a case being handled by the Justice Department. There were too many rules and too much protocol that would have to be broken.

She placed the receiver back in the cradle, her head pounding with fatigue, her mouth dry with fear. Being alone had never bothered her. She enjoyed her solitude.

Right now, she wanted company.

She wanted a friend who would pat her on the back and tell her everything was going to be okay. She wanted a familiar voice on the other end of the phone line, reminding her that God had everything under control, that she was not alone and that there were people praying for her and anxiously awaiting her return.

She couldn't think of one person who could do that for her.

That was sad.

It was more than sad, it was discouraging and heartbreaking and horrible that she had put so much time and energy and passion into a job rather than her relationships.

"I want a do-over, Lord," she whispered, her voice raspy and raw with fatigue. She and Mac had been going all night, running and then driving. He had fled his home and everything he knew and loved to help her. She knew he was being paid, but there were plenty of people who wouldn't have been willing to risk their lives for a job.

A door opened, the soft creak of old hinges making the hair on the back of her neck stand on end. She walked to the door and looked out the peephole. There was no one in her field of vision. No shadow on the wall across the hall. The soft thud of a door closing made her jump back. Someone had been in the hall and had gone into the room next door. Another guest?

She wanted to believe that.

The place was old and run-down, but it was inexpensive. There were probably plenty of people who would want to stay there. Still, with so many empty rooms, why put guests so close together?

She tiptoed to the door that separated adjacent rooms, pressing her ear to it, her thundering heartbeat making it nearly impossible to hear anything.

The knob wiggled, and she jumped back.

The bolt was still in place but as she watched, the lock popped, the knob turned.

She dove for the bed, scrambling over it and diving to the floor on the other side, expecting gunshots to shatter the eerie quiet.

"Anna," Mac whispered.

She popped back up, saw him peering out from the crack in the partially open door.

"What are you doing? You scared ten years off my life," she hissed, rushing to pull the bolt.

"Turn off the lights," he responded, stepping into the room and rushing to the window to unlock and open it. She thought they were going to climb out, but he grabbed her hand, yanking her with him as he closed the bathroom door and hurried back into the room next door.

He closed the door, using a multitool to lock it from the outside. Then closed the second door, bolting and locking it.

"What's going on?" she whispered.

He pressed a finger to his lips and shook his head, gesturing for her to follow him across the threadbare rug. Like the other room, this one had a door to an adjoining room. It was opened, and he led her through, closing and locking both doors. She planned to ask questions, but his hands were resting on her shoulders, his silvery-blue eyes staring straight into hers.

He didn't tell her to stay quiet.

He didn't have to.

They stood like that for several minutes, her breathing calming, her heartbeat slowing. The weight of his hands comforting. She didn't know how it happened. One minute, she was standing a foot away, staring into his eyes. The next, she was inches from his chest, his hands sliding down her shoulders and resting on her back.

"Shh," he whispered, pressing her head to his chest, his fingers combing through her hair.

She closed her eyes, giving in for a moment, allowing herself to relax against him, to let him offer the support she had been craving. It felt right to be there, comfortable in a way few things in her life had. She had always felt as if she were swimming against the tide, fighting to find her place in the world. She had thought that a good job, a nice home and a network of friends and coworkers would give her the feeling of belonging, but they had only fed her emptiness. Her marriage had done the same. She had yearned for a place where she felt like she was home, and she had searched for it in dozens of different ways—reaching out to church groups, joining book clubs, working extra hours to make herself indispensable.

Only she hadn't been.

Her supervisor hadn't been distraught when she had announced that she was taking a leave of absence. He had been understanding of the situation she was in, and he had assured her that she could return to her job after the trial, but he hadn't seemed worried about the case load she had been carrying. By the time she'd left the hospital and met with him, he had another attorney lined up to take over.

The FBI was doing just fine without her.

Her friends were doing just fine.

Her church groups and book clubs were doing fine.

She wanted just one person in her life who wouldn't be fine if she were gone.

Voices carried in from the hall. Men. Maybe a woman, too. She could hear them talking but not what was being said. She pulled back, looking into Mac's face.

"Police," he mouthed.

She nodded, tense again, ready for someone to knock on the door and barrel in. Boots thudded on the floor outside their room, the soft squeak of leather shoes reminding her of the courthouse the night of the shooting and the soft creak of leather holsters and polished shoes as the police escorted their prisoner outside.

She was trembling, her teeth chattering with the force of her fear and the memories.

Mac's arms curved around her, his hands

sliding under her coat and smoothing circles along her spine. She tried to focus on that and not allow herself to drift into the past. She'd had flashbacks before. She had dealt with the panic by running. Now she was trapped, unable to do anything but stand where she was and pray she wasn't pulled so far into past terror that she forgot where she was and what was at stake.

Anna was panicking, her hands fisted at her sides, her breathing shallow. He could feel the terror rolling off her in waves of useless energy that he thought had more to do with her past and less to do with their current situation. He didn't want to be caught by the police, but if they were, it wasn't the end of the road for either of them. They weren't criminals. They had done nothing wrong. If River had called in APBs on them, it would have been because they were in possible danger. Not because they were wanted.

Unless he was in Moreno's pocket.

Then, he had called in for help locating them because he needed to finish the job he had been paid to do.

He frowned, smoothing a hand down Anna's spine and pressing her head to his chest. She was wound up tight, her body so taut she was trembling. He could hear the police knocking on a door, the soft clink of keys as they unlocked it. They weren't going in with guns drawn. They weren't expecting trouble. They were going to find an empty room and an open window. Let them think what they wanted about that. He had been back to the car and removed the remainder of the cash from the lockbox. He didn't think he would need it. His plan was to return to Sweet Valley as soon as Seamus arrived. They weren't going to find answers cowering in a motel room, and he wasn't going to leave Anna behind so he could search himself.

The voices grew closer and then receded. No stress in them. No real sense of urgency. They were looking for possible victims of a crime. Possible witnesses to it. That wasn't a surprise to Mac. He had been expecting and prepping for it from the moment he had left Anna in the room.

She was still shaking, still tense, her muscles taut with the effort to keep her terror under control.

"It's okay," he said quietly, his hands stroking the length of her back. His goal was to ground her in the moment, hold her there instead of letting her mind jump to the past. He'd had flashbacks. He knew how real the danger could feel. If she started screaming, they'd be discovered. Not the end of the world, but not in his plans. He wanted freedom to return to the ranch as quickly as possible. The sooner he pulled the security footage and saw who had entered Anna's cabin, the happier he would be. He had a ranch to run. He had people depending on him. He also had Anna's life in his hands. His choices, decisions he made could mean the difference between her survival and her death.

She pulled back, her hands shaking as she dragged her hair from the ponytail holder and scraped it into a messy bun at the back of her neck. A few strands lay against her neck and slid across her shoulders, and she pulled the coat tight and tried to button it. She was still breathing unevenly, her pulse pounding rapidly in the hollow of her throat, her hands shaking violently.

He brushed them away, buttoning the coat quickly even though he had no intention of leaving the hotel until Seamus arrived. If being buttoned into heavy wool calmed her, he was all for it.

She didn't meet his eyes as she pulled the collar of the coat around her ears and then smoothed it down again.

"Well, that was fun," she murmured, offering a tired smile as she glanced toward the window. The curtains were wide open, the parking lot clearly visible. "I should close those."

"Not yet." He snagged the back of the

coat to hold her in place. "The police might notice and come back."

"I guess the old guy at the desk doesn't really mind his own business."

"Did you think he would?"

"Every once in a while, I have hope that a person is really what he says," she replied, her body still trembling but her voice clear.

He wanted to pull her back into his arms, absorb the tremors that were wracking her body and tell her again that everything would be okay.

"Every once in a while, a person is," he replied, edging her closer to the wall, afraid the police would walk past the window and see them there.

"Maybe." She tucked a strand of hair behind her ear, her hand shaking. He should have left it alone, gone on with the morning and pretended he didn't see that she was still struggling.

That was probably what she wanted.

It was probably what he should want.

He didn't need to complicate the situation by letting emotions come into play. Not his or hers. But he had known her for seven months. He'd watched her adjust to life on the ranch, he'd seen how she'd fit herself into the community there, and he had been intrigued by that. Most of the guests who visited Sweet Valley Dude Ranch were there to escape hectic urban and suburban lives. They weren't there to get their hands dirty. They wanted the experience of ranch life minus all the hard stuff. The witnesses he'd allowed to stay and work on the ranch had been the same. Some were low-level criminals who had decided to come clean and make a fresh start. Others were family members of criminals. A few had been victims. None had been like Anna—eager to get involved, energetic and enthusiastic about the assigned work.

He had admired her work ethic and positive outlook from the day she had arrived on the ranch. He hadn't taken the time to tell her that. His life was busy. The ranch demanded all his time and attention, but people were important too. Their well-being also needed to be a priority.

He wrapped his hand around hers, stilling the tremors and offering what he hoped was a reassuring smile. "Everything is fine. Even if the police had found us, we wouldn't have been in immediate danger."

"I know," she said quietly. He didn't hear fear in her voice. He heard defeat.

"It gets better," he said, speaking into the silence, filling it with words he knew were useless. This was a road she had to walk at her own pace. All the platitudes and encouragement in the world couldn't change that.

"Does it?" she moved back, her hands dropping away as she paced to the bathroom door and opened it. She stood staring into the dark interior, her back to Mac. Maybe she didn't want him to see the fear that was still in her eyes.

"It takes time, but yes."

"How much time?" she asked, turning to face him again.

"For me? It's been nearly a decade. I still have nightmares. Once in a while, I have a panic attack or a flashback."

"From your time in the military?"

"I lost friends in the military. I held one of my best friends as he lay dying after the IED explosion that ended my career." He said it casually, but it still hurt. Even after all this time. The fact that he had let months pass without touching base with Seamus bothered him a lot. Their bond had been tight, but it had been forged in steel the day they had watched Scott Handler die.

"I'm sorry, Mac. I know that doesn't help, but I am."

"And I'm sorry your life got turned upside down by Moreno and his hired hit man. I'm sure you'd rather have spent the past six months in Boston."

"I don't know. I was working too hard in

Boston. One of those hamsters on a wheel, running fast and getting nowhere."

"Becoming a defense attorney for the FBI isn't getting nowhere."

She shrugged, the loose strands of her hair sliding across her nape. "It isn't necessarily getting where I wanted to be, either."

"Where did you want to be?" he asked.

"I wanted a family. Kids. The house in the suburbs. All the things that I thought would come along once I had the job." She smiled. "I have a one-bedroom apartment in a nice area of Boston and a potted fern that I gave to my neighbor before I left town, so life isn't bad. It's just not exactly what I planned."

"You still have plenty of time to work on those plans."

"Not if I die."

"I won't let you die."

"Keeping me alive goes above and beyond the buddy code of conduct," she said with a wry smile. "As a matter of fact, I'd understand if you headed back to the ranch and left me here to fend for myself."

"I'm pretty sure keeping you alive is in the code," he replied, smiling in return.

"Is this our first argument, Mac?" she asked, raising an eyebrow, all the terror and anxiety gone from her face and her eyes.

"How about we discuss that at a later date?" He pulled out the phone he'd used to call Seamus. He needed to let him know what room they were in and warn him that the police were prowling the area.

"That's what every man says when he plans to never discuss something again," she quipped.

"I'm not every man, so how about we discuss it over dinner after this is over?"

"Dinner that I cook in the ranch kitchen and serve to you and a dozen guests and a couple dozen ranch hands?" She laughed, her eyes glowing with amusement.

"That *I* cook," he replied.

"You cook?"

"Of course."

"Is there anything you don't do?"

"Plenty. We can discuss that over dinner, too." He had been trying to lighten her mood and get her mind off her fear, but he liked the idea of having dinner with Anna.

"Sounds too good to pass up," she murmured, the amusement fading from her eyes.

"Then don't."

"Don't what?"

"Pass it up."

"Did I say I was going to?"

"You were thinking about it."

"I mentioned that I was married before, right?"

"What does that have to do with dinner?"

"You're not the kind of guy many women would want to walk away from."

"I have an ex who proves otherwise."

"You were married?"

"Engaged."

"That's not the same."

"No, but that doesn't mean I don't understand what it's like to love someone and then watch them walk away." He didn't offer more information. The relationship had ended years ago. It wasn't something he spent much time thinking about, and he certainly didn't waste time talking about it.

"I'm sorry things didn't work out."

"Yeah. Me, too. I thought I'd have the family and kids, too."

"I guess we both still have time for those things."

"I guess we do," he replied, and for the first time in longer than he could remember, he wondered if there was room in his life for those old dreams to spring to life.

It was something he wanted to think about. Something he was open to. If the right woman came along.

As he dialed Seamus's number and waited for his friend to pick up, he couldn't help wondering if she already had.

TEN

Seamus Murphy arrived silently, slipping into the room through the side door rather than the hallway. A few inches shorter than Mac with black hair and vivid green eyes, he had a lean runner's build and a hard-edged gaze that would have made Anna fidget if she hadn't spent most of her adult life working in the court system and dealing with law enforcement officers.

"Thanks for coming, brother," Mac said, giving him a side hug and a hard pat on the back.

"You'd have done the same for me. If I ever needed help, but we both know that rarely happens." He smiled, offering Anna a firm handshake. "Ma'am, I'm Seamus Murphy. Shay to my friends."

"Annalise Rivers. Anna to everyone in Texas." His smile broadened.

"Anna, then. I wasn't expecting Mac to have a friend with him, but it's pleasure to meet you."

"I wish it were under better circumstances," she responded.

"Yes. The circumstances are a little less than idea." He glanced around the room. "You two ready to get out of here? My Jeep is parked out front. You can fill me in on what's going on once we're on the road."

"Heading back to the ranch?" Mac asked, tossing the phone he had used on the bedside table and leaving it there.

"Is that the plan?"

"Yes."

"Then let's go."

Shay didn't ask questions as they stepped into the hall. The two men flanked Annalise, shoulders brushing hers as they all marched past the check-in desk and out into the parking lot. There was no trying to hide, no darting behind cars or sprinting away. They were leaving in plain sight of anyone who cared to look, and Mac seemed fine with that.

She felt exposed, anxious and worried.

She'd agreed that going back to the ranch made sense. They needed to get the security footage from the cameras near her cabin if they were going to figure out who had placed the tracking device in her pedometer. Whoever it was had probably been paid a hefty sum of money to do it.

Desperation made people do desperate things.

It was possible her betrayer would become a murderer with the right motivation. She hated to think that. She didn't want to believe that any of the people she had met on the ranch would hurt her.

Shay's Jeep was parked near the curb, the engine still running. He opened the back door, and she climbed in, her pulse racing uncomfortably. This might be just another day for Mac and Shay, but it wasn't for Annalise. She worked with FBI agents. Not hardened criminals. She defended them from false accusations. She spent hours in her office doing research and prepping for trial. She never knowingly walked into dangerous situations. She wasn't excited about doing it now.

But if that was what it was going to take to plug the leak and stop Moreno, that's what she would have to do.

"What about the SUV?" she asked as Mac climbed in the front passenger seat.

"I'll send a ranch hand to get it and return it to Linda. For now, we're safer staying together."

She was safer.

They were not.

The closer they got to her, the more danger they were putting themselves in. That was something she couldn't forget as she settled into the leather seat. It weighed on her mind, caused her to wonder if she were making a terrible mistake. If something happened to Mac or Shay because of her, she didn't think she could ever forgive herself.

Shay pulled out of the parking lot. Mac was filling him in, explaining the situation without going into details about how they'd gotten into it. Annalise appreciated that he didn't point out that she had left the safety of the ranch. She appreciated him, but that didn't mean she should have agreed to dinner. She had almost taken it back, almost told him that dinner wasn't a good idea. Then he had smiled, and all she had been able to think about were all the reasons it would be.

Mac was a good guy.

She knew that.

And maybe she was ready to meet a good guy, to go to dinner with him, to find out if one dinner led to another. She just wasn't sure her heart would ever be ready to be hurt again.

The trip back to the ranch took less time than Annalise wanted it to. As they pulled through up to the gates that led onto the property, she scanned the area, searching for signs that they were being watched. A bullet didn't need to be fired close-range to kill someone. A good sniper could take someone out from hundreds of yards away.

Seamus punched in the gate code as Mac recited it.

The gates swung open, closing behind them as they drove through. She should have felt safer, but she imagined being watched from one of the hills outside the property.

"You've got security cameras and fences, but the area around the ranch has plenty of places for snipers to hide," Shay said as if he had read her mind.

"The houses are far enough back be out of range."

"Good planning."

"I didn't plan it. My great-grandfather did, but it's worked out nicely."

"It's a great spread, Mac. I should have come out for a visit long before now." Shay followed the long driveway past several pastures and up to the front door of the main house. The one-story brick home sprawled across a lush yard, the U-shaped building surrounded by fruit trees and a white picket fence.

From the first day she had arrived at Sweet Valley Ranch, Annalise had thought the house was the stereotypical ranch home. Beautiful but understated, well-cared-for but not ostentatious. She had only been inside few times. Once during her interview for the job as assistant cook. The second time, to help the housekeeper carry in cleaning supplies. She'd been there for an employee Christmas party and for a Thanksgiving meal. Other than that, she had spent her time in the kitchen, the dining hall or her cabin.

She followed Mac and Shay inside, trying to ignore the voice in her head screaming that she wasn't safe, that she would have been better off staying alone in the seedy motel than returning to the place where a traitor was hiding. Mac had assured her that she would be safe, and she had to believe him. Otherwise, she'd start running and she wouldn't stop.

A small foyer opened into a central family room, a huge stone fireplace taking up one wall. The house had probably been built in the fifties, but it had been well maintained, the hardwood floors still gleaming, the walls painted a neutral gray that contrasted with the bright white trim. Area rugs and a leather sectional made the large room inviting. During the Christmas party, the room had been decorated with a Christmas tree, garland and lights. A nativity set had been placed on a table in the center of the room, and guests had moved around it as they'd chatted and laughed.

Annalise glanced at Mac, wondering if he'd had any part of decorating for the holidays. Probably. He seemed to take part in all the activities on the ranch. He was often covered in dust and dirt, heading in from the field, the setting sun glinting in his hair. She had found herself watching him more often than she wanted to admit.

He was eye-catching, like a stained-glass window in a Victorian home or a daisy in a field of dandelions.

A daisy in field of dandelions?

She was obviously exhausted and in serious need of sleep. She wasn't a flowery kind of girl. She liked books and chipped vases and old things that people had used hundreds of years before she was born. She did not spend her time thinking about fields of daises and dandelions. She certainly didn't waste it mooning over a man. Moreno had discovered her hiding place. He had sent men to kill her. That was where all her attention needed to be.

"What now?" she asked, suddenly filled with the need to *do* something.

The men had been talking quietly on the opposite side of the room, Mac leaning against the fireplace mantel, the five-o-clock shadow on his face giving him a scruffy, tough appearance. He met her eyes, offering a quick smile that made butterflies take flight in her stomach and a dozen dead dreams spring to life in her heart.

This wasn't good.

It couldn't be good.

First, because she wasn't looking for a relationship.

Second, because Mac lived in Texas, she lived in Boston, and one day they would be living thousands of miles apart.

Third, because…

She couldn't think of another reason. Not one that made sense. She couldn't tell herself that she didn't want to be hurt again, because she didn't believe that Mac would ever hurt her. Not intentionally. She couldn't say that he wasn't the kind of guy she was attracted to, because she was obviously very attracted to exactly his type.

Her cheeks heated at the thought, and she glanced away.

"I'm going to have you stay in one of the guest rooms tonight. We'll go to your cabin and grab some of your things after I make a few phone calls."

"I'm not going to hide in a bedroom while you and Shay take care of my problems for me," she said, her voice a little sharper than she intended. Being attracted to him made her feel vulnerable. It wasn't a feeling she was used to. It wasn't one she liked.

"I don't recall saying that you would be," he responded calmly.

"Right. Sorry. I'm a little on edge."

"You're very quick to apologize," he commented, grabbing a few logs from behind the fireplace and crouching down to set them in place.

"When I'm wrong," she replied. There were matches in an old cigar box on the mantel. She grabbed a couple and handed them to him.

"Why would you apologize otherwise?" He placed tinder in with the logs and lit a match, tossing it on top of the pile. Flames licked at the dry wood, crackling happily as he straightened and met her eyes.

There was a smudge of dirt on his cheeks

and dark circles beneath his eyes. A thin white scar stretched from his hairline down to his ear. Another sliced across the column of his neck near the jugular vein. She tried not to think about him wounded, bleeding, holding his dying friend, but of course, that was where her mind went. To Mac the way he must have been when he'd returned home after his time in the military—wounded and scarred, haunted by memories that no one should have.

"Anna?" he prodded, studying her as carefully as she was studying him. The chemistry between them stretched like a taut cord, pulling her closer to his arms.

She had been there before, hugged close to his chest, listening to the comforting thud of his heart.

She backed up. "You said you wanted to make some phone calls?"

"I want to see if River found the guys who were after you last night. I also need to call Daniel and check in again. He needs to be working on his end to find the leak and seal it."

"If the leak is on his end," Seamus said. He had a cell phone in hand and was dialing a number. He pressed it to his ear, striding to the French doors that led out onto a patio.

He stepped outside, closing the door so they couldn't hear the conversation.

"What's he doing?" she asked, trying not to look into Mac's eyes. She needed to focus on solving her problems. Not making new ones for herself. Dinner with Mac was one thing. Falling for him? That was something else entirely.

But she was going to fall.

If she wasn't very careful.

If she didn't guard her heart.

If she didn't do everything possible to not fall.

"Calling some associates in Boston who might be hearing rumors on the street."

"Rumors?"

"About who might have been paid to come out here to find you."

"Right." She crossed the room, putting distance between them and trying to clear her head so she could think.

"What's wrong, Anna?" Mac said quietly.

She met his eyes. Just exactly like she knew she shouldn't. He had followed her, and they were so close she could see flecks of silver and blue in his irises, so close she could count the tiny smile lines that fanned out from the corners of his eyes.

So close she could have reached out and touched him if she'd wanted to.

She wanted to, but she shouldn't.

They were two people brought together by unusual circumstances. When circumstances changed, they would go back to their lives.

Wouldn't they?

"I'm worried."

"That's understandable. You've got some very dangerous people very unhappy with you. If worry makes you cautious, I'm all for it."

"I'm not worried about that. I mean, I *am* worried about that, but I'm also worried about you." She'd always been a straight shooter. She didn't believe in hedging around something. If it needed to be said, she said it with as much diplomacy and kindness as she could manage. But saying what was on her mind and in her heart regarding Mac? That wasn't as easy as she wanted it to be.

"I know how to take care of myself. You don't have to worry about that."

"Of course, I do. You and Seamus are risking your lives to keep me safe, and if something were to happen—"

"It would be because we understood the risks and accepted them. Not because of you."

"That wouldn't change the fact that you were injured because of me. I could never forgive myself if that happened."

"Never is a long time."

"And death is a permanent state of being.

You have a ranch and a bunch of people working on it that are relying on you to keep things running."

"I will try very hard not to die, Anna. Does that help?" he said with a hint of amusement in his eyes that made her want to do exactly what she knew she shouldn't and reach out to trace the lines near his eyes and smooth his hair into place.

"That isn't the only thing I'm worried about. I'm worried about the way I feel when we're together. About what's going to happen after this is over, if I make the mistake of falling for you." There. She'd said it.

"Why would it be a mistake?" he asked.

She wasn't sure what response she had expected, but it wasn't that.

"That's a good question," she replied. "I need a little time to think of an answer."

"If that's the case, maybe the answer isn't one you need to spend time worrying about," he said, tucking a lose strand of hair behind her ear, his fingers calloused and rough, his touch gentle. She lost herself for a moment. Lost every thought about how dangerous it would be to fall in love with someone who lived a world apart from her.

"Maybe not," she murmured, leaning toward him as he leaned toward her. His lips touched hers, a gentle caress that reminded her of all the good things in the world. Sunshine. Laughter. Family on Christmas morning.

When he moved back, she wanted to step toward him again, to wrap her arms around his waist and bury her face in the scratchy wool of his coat. To allow herself, for just a little while, to believe she would always find safety in his arms.

A hard rap at the door pulled her from the moment, and she jumped back, swinging toward the sound.

"Looks like I'm not going to have to call River," Mac said, gesturing toward the large bay window and the police cruiser parked out front as he walked to the door and opened it.

* * *

River paced the room, his frustration and anger obvious in every step he took and every word he didn't say.

"I don't know what you were thinking," he said, his words clipped, his expression hard. He had been to the ranch hundreds of times. Always as a friend. They'd sat on the patio and talked about life a couple times a week every summer for as long as Mac had been running the place.

"I was thinking that people wanted Anna dead. They wanted me dead and sitting in your office waiting for them to find us wasn't a good plan."

"And you didn't think to inform me of that?"

"I wasn't thinking much of anything except that I needed to get somewhere safe and go through my options."

"You were worried I was involved," River said. There was no accusation in his voice. It was a statement.

"I didn't think you were involved, but

I wasn't taking chances. Someone on the ranch or in town tipped off Moreno. Until I know who, it pays to be cautious."

"I can't fault you for that, but I don't appreciate having to chase your trail all over town," River muttered. "Briarwood relies on my deputies to keep things safe, and we're not doing a good job of it if we're all off on a wild-goose chase trying to save your hide."

"Has it occurred to you that one of your deputies could be involved?" Seamus inserted himself into the conversation, his relaxed demeanor belying the sharpness in his gaze. Like Mac, he didn't trust many people. He certainly wasn't going to trust a stranger.

"It's occurred to me that anyone in this town or on the ranch could be. I've already run phone records on my deputies. So far, I haven't seen anything suspicious."

"You have those printed out?" Seamus asked.

"I do, but I'm not handing them off to

anyone. They're my responsibility. I'll finish going through them."

"Understood, Sheriff, but many hands make light work. Or so my grandmother always said," Seamus responded, his Irish brogue thick, his expression hard.

"Your grandmother was right, so how about we work as a team to bring Moreno's hit men down?" River responded. "My deputies have been patrolling town and the area around Sweet Valley Ranch. So far, they've found nothing. No abandoned vehicles. No signs of one. I was hoping we might find some tire tracks, but we've come up empty."

"They moved the vehicle before the snow blew in. Or, they're on a side road that hasn't been searched." Mac could think of a few dozen dirt roads that wound through the area. Most of them were nearly impassable this time of year, but someone who wanted to stay hidden would be highly motivated to try.

"There are too many roads to search effectively in vehicles. We might be able to get the state police to bring out a helicopter, but not until the weather clears."

"Right now, I want to focus on footage from my security cameras," Mac said, explaining the tracking device he had found attached to the pedometer on Anna's shoe.

"The shoes have stayed in your cabin when they're not on your feet?" Seamus asked.

"Where else would they be?" she responded. She looked tired, her face pale, her eyes shadowed. Mac refused to allow himself to think about how smooth her skin was, how sweet her lips.

He shouldn't have kissed her, but he didn't regret it.

"On your porch? Airing out?"

"I always bring them inside, and I always lock my door. Whoever planted the tracking device had a key or picked the lock."

"The security camera should give us some answers," Mac said. "How about we grab your things, Anna? You can rest while we go through the footage."

"We all could probably use some rest," she replied.

"Or some coffee," Seamus intoned. "You have any around here, Mac?"

"I'll brew a pot after we get back. The security footage is on the main hard drive in my office. That's also where I keep the spare keys for the guest and employee cabins."

"Do you have a security camera in there?" Seamus asked as they stepped outside. The storm had died, the clouds receding to reveal a pristine blue sky. Sunlight glinted off the ice-coated foliage, creating a winter wonderland outside the front door.

Mac had enjoyed summers at the ranch when he was a kid.

As an adult, he loved the slower pace of winter, the crisp mornings and cold nights. Firelight playing on the walls of the great room as he sipped coffee after a long day.

He had kept the property the way his

great-grandfather and grandfather had built it, adding a few small log cabins to entice city dwellers to the wonder of ranch life. There was a bunkhouse a half mile from the main house where ranch hands stayed during the hectic calving season. A few employee cabins were nearby, rough-cut log structures that had been built to house the cooking staff and ranch foreman. Back when his grandfather had been running cattle, the business had made enough to survive but not enough to pay well. Free room and board had enticed hardworking farmers who had fallen on tough times and needed to rebuild their lives.

Since Mac had taken over, the dude ranch had become the bread and butter of the operation. Guests were willing to pay good money to spend a week living on the ranch, riding the trails on pack horses that had been trained to accommodate inexperienced riders, eating food by a bonfire at night and sleeping in posh log cabins that offered all the amenities they were used to at home. Between that and the cattle business, Mac was able to pay his employees decent salaries. Most of them chose to live in town. After nearly two decades of living in ranch housing, even Lucas had opted out. He had purchased a house in town the previous year, and he'd seemed happy with the change.

That had left an empty cabin. When Anna arrived, he'd assigned it to her. Like the bunkhouse, it was a half mile away from the main property, a sturdy structure with two bedrooms, a small kitchen and a living area. They could have walked there easily, but he didn't want to take chances. Until they knew who the traitor was, he couldn't count on the ranch being a safe place for Anna to hide.

They rode in Seamus's Jeep, bouncing over the dirt road that had been worn into the earth from decades of vehicles driving back and forth from the ranch house to the employee cabins. The cattle had been fed and let out to range. He could see them on a distant hill, dark bodies against the icy landscape. One of the men had a tractor out in the west field where alfalfa would soon be planted. A stallion pranced along the fence line nearby, a few mares nuzzling frozen blades of grass.

This was home.

A place he had never expected to love. He had been keen on adventure, amped up and ready to blow Texas and explore the world. He hadn't had any intention of returning to Houston where he had grown up or to the ranch where he had spent so many of his summers. Not for any amount of time anyway.

He had planned to make a career of the military, then retire to Florida or the East Coast. Somewhere more urban and full of life. If he hadn't been injured, that is probably what he would have done.

God had had other plans.

Mac couldn't say he was sorry. He had found his place on Sweet Valley Ranch. He had learned to love the flow of the seasons and the rhythm of life there. Even if he could go back and change things, he wouldn't have.

"Which one?" Seamus asked as they reached the cabins. The bunkhouse was farther away, a long porch with several chairs and small tables facing the direction of the rising sun. The other cabins were closer together, each with a tiny backyard and space to park a car.

"Mine's the one with the red Chevy in front of it," Anna said, pointing to the larger of the five cabins. It was the only one with two bedrooms, its front porch just a little wider than the others. She had potted plants flanking the steps and flower boxes hanging from the porch railing. She had whitewashed the old wood a few months after she'd moved in, asking permission in a quick email that he'd responded to in kind. He hadn't expected her to make the place better. It had been empty for several months before she'd moved in, the wood floors dinged from decades of booted feet, the fireplace mantel blackened from hundreds of fires.

She had cleaned it up and made it home.

At least, that's what Stacey had told him. Stacey had been a fixture on the ranch for nearly as long as Lucas, cooking meals for the ranch hands for nearly a decade before Mac had taken over the business. When he had presented the idea of a dude ranch to his employees, she had been the most enthusiastic, jumping at the opportunity to create meals for a wider audience.

He loved her like an aunt, and he didn't want to believe she could have betrayed his trust, but she had befriended Anna. She had certainly been inside the cabin many times in the past seven months.

Seamus parked in front of the cabin, and Anna jumped out.

"It's good to be back," she said as she hurried up the steps. She paused at the top. "That's funny."

"What?" he asked, nearly bumping into her.

"That potted plant." She gestured to one

standing beside the door, a tall bush that he thought she might have decorated with lights during the holidays.

"What about it?"

"It's usually on the back stoop. I wonder why it's here." She took a step forward, but his hair was standing on end, adrenaline shooting through his blood.

He grabbed her waist, pulling her backward and off the steps, diving onto the ground as the world exploded in a hail of thunder and fire.

ELEVEN

One minute she was reaching for her favorite potted plant, and the next she was lying on the ground, Mac's deadweight pressing her down. She tried to turn her head so she could see what was happening and understand what had occurred. Black smoke rose from crater where the porch had once been. Red blood stained the ground beside her, and Mac was on top of her. Limp and quiet.

"Mac!" She tried to scream his name, but smoke clogged her throat and stole the breath from her lungs. She shoved against the frozen ground, twisting so that she could pull herself out from beneath Mac.

He was unconscious, blood seeping from a gash in the back of his head. Fire lapped at the old log cabin, consuming it at a frantic pace. Embers floated to the ground, catching bits of dead leaves on fire. She had to move. She had to get Mac away from the carnage.

She grabbed him beneath his arms, dragging him one slow step at a time. Blood dripped from her shoulder. She must have been hit with shrapnel, too. She didn't have time to assess the damage. She didn't have time to think about what had happened and why.

She had to keep moving away from the expanding fire and the shooting flames. Heat sizzled in the air, crackling around her in a snapping frenzy that made her body shake.

"Just keep going," she muttered, pulling Mac another few feet.

"We need to move faster," someone said.

Mac was lifted from the ground and tossed over Seamus's shoulder.

"Come on! We've got no idea if there's another explosion coming!" He grabbed her hand, dragging her with him as he sprinted away from the burning building.

"Where's River?" she shouted, her voice hoarse from smoke and fear, her body throbbing from the impact of the explosion. If Mac hadn't pulled her away, if he hadn't covered her with his body, she would be dead.

"I thought he ran," Seamus responded, setting Mac down gently, tapping his cheek. "You in there, brother?"

Mac moaned but didn't open his eyes. Blood still seeped from his head, soaking into the ground at an alarming rate.

"I don't see him," Anna said, slipping out of her coat and using it to staunch the flow of blood. She could see a deep laceration in his scalp. He needed medical treatment immediately.

Ranch hands were running across the field, shouting in alarm as the fire rose into the pristine sky.

"Stay here. Do not leave this area. Do not leave his side. Anyone does anything you don't like, shoot him. You do know how to use a gun, right?" Seamus pulled one from a holster beneath his coat and handed it to her.

"Yes." She took it with her right hand, her left hand pressing the coat against Mac's head. He was too pale, and too quiet, and she was back in time, lying on the courthouse steps, staring into the blank-eyed gaze of the prosecuting attorney.

"We've got to hold it together until help comes. You hear what I'm saying?" Seamus gave her a gentle shake, his voice thick with Irish brogue, his eyes cold with fury.

"I'm fine. I'll be fine. Go find River," she said, and she meant it.

She wasn't going to panic.

She was going to focus with the same precision she used when prepping for a trial. She kept the gun in her hand, safety on, barrel pointed to the ground as she checked Mac's pulse. It was thready and quick, his breathing shallow.

"Dear Lord have mercy on all of us," a

woman shouted, her voice tinged with all the panic Anna was feeling but could not give in to. "What happened? What could have possibly happened?"

Stacey appeared beside her, dropping down in a puddle of denim and flannel, her salt-and-pepper hair pulled into the snood she wore when she cooked.

"Honey, what happened?" she repeated, her voice calmer, her gaze on Mac and then on the gun.

"There was an explosion."

"Yes. I see that. But how? Did the gas range explode?"

"The plant exploded," she said, coughing on the words, her shoulder throbbing, her lungs burning, her gaze still on Mac. He hadn't moved, and she was growing more worried by the second.

"Mac," Stacey said, leaning over him, checking his pulse and patting his cheek. "We need an ambulance. Did anyone call an ambulance?"

"Yes, ma'am," one of the younger ranch

hands said. Anna thought his name was Trent or Trey. He knelt beside them.

"I'm a volunteer with fire department. EMT, too. How about we stabilize his neck? Make sure that we don't do more damage to him?"

"I dragged him across the road, and his friend carried him here," Anna admitted, horrified by the thought of Mac being paralyzed. Of everything he had worked so hard to achieve being ruined because he had tried to protect her.

"You had to. That fire is raging, and there was no knowing if the gas line would cause another explosion."

"We need to cut the gas to this part of the ranch," Stacey said worriedly, her dark eyes scanning the crowd that had gathered.

"Lucas was out in the far west pasture last time I saw him. He's probably making his way here. But don't worry. I turned off the gas as soon as I saw the flames," the young man said.

He'd stripped off his coat. Anna thought

he'd use it to cover Mac. Instead, he draped it around her shoulders.

She started to shrug it off and use it for Mac.

He stopped her. "You're shivering and in shock. Keep it on. The ambulance is here. He'll be at the hospital and under medical care soon."

"River may need help, too," she murmured, the horror of what had happened finally beginning to register. The cabin had nearly been consumed by flames. A group of ranch hands had pulled hoses from outbuildings and hooked them to spigots outside nearby structures. The streams of water that were dousing the flames were like a drop of water in a volcano. They fizzled and evaporated, the heat from the inferno driving back the men and women who were trying to douse it.

A fire truck screamed up the road, sirens blaring and lights flashing. It pulled to a stop near an old fire hydrant that Anna had noticed but never thought much about. An ambulance sped up behind it. Paramedics jumped out and ran toward them, medical bags slapping their sides.

Smoke billowed across the road and up into the sky, black clouds that seemed to reflect the heart of the person who had planted the bomb meant to kill her.

Had it killed Mac?

River?

She glanced toward the cabin. Seamus was rushing away from the burning building, River over his shoulder in a fireman carry. The sheriff's leg was twisted at an odd angle, his face pale, his eyes wide open and filled with fury.

He was alive. Injured, but alive.

So was Mac.

For now.

She prayed he wasn't gravely injured as the paramedics rushed in and urged her away. Two leaned over her, asking questions she tried to answer. The words were in her head, but they came out jumbled and frantic, the panic that she had been holding back suddenly rearing up again.

A police officer appeared at her side. He knelt next to her, his dark eyes filled with concern.

"Ma'am, I'm going to need you to put the weapon down," he said gently.

She nodded numbly, setting the handgun down, her hand shaking, her body trembling.

She wanted to believe it was over.

That this would be the end of the terror, but until they knew who had placed the bomb, until that person was apprehended, she didn't think anyone on the ranch was safe.

It was her fault.

She felt the heaviness of that as Mac was lifted onto a stretcher and rolled to the waiting ambulance. She jumped to her feet, refusing to stop when the paramedics cautioned her to remain still.

She didn't care about the wound in her shoulder.

She didn't care that she was dripping blood onto the ground.

All she cared about was making sure that Mac was okay.

Mac woke to the steady beep of machines and the quiet hiss of oxygen being pumped through a hose. For a moment, he thought he was at his grandmother's hospital bed, holding her hand as she slipped into a coma. Then he heard the quiet murmur of voices, felt a cold palm lying against his knuckles, realized he was the one in the bed.

His eyes flew open, and he sat up, shoving aside blankets that were piled on top of him.

"Whoa, brother," Seamus said, pressing him back. "Not so fast. You've been here for two days. No sense in trying to take the world by storm today."

"Two days?" he murmured, his throat scratchy, the oxygen tubes pumping air into his nose irritating him. He pulled them away, tossing them onto the bed, still trying to figure out how he had ended up in a hospital bed with Seamus standing over him.

"We were really worried about you," Anna said. "*I* was worried about you." She was sitting beside him, her hand resting on his, her palm cool and dry. There was a bruise on her cheek and a long scratch on her neck.

He frowned, images rushing through his mind. The cabin. The plant. Knowing before he really knew what was going to happen. Dragging Anna off the steps, diving for cover.

"Was anyone hurt?" he asked, sitting up again. There was an IV in his arm and heart monitor attached to his chest. He had a pounding headache and an aching need for water, but other than that, he figured he was ready to get up and go back to the ranch.

"You were hurt," Anna pointed out, standing up and trying to push him back onto the pillows. "And River's leg is broken. He's not happy about it. The cabin is destroyed, and I can't tell you how sorry I am that I brought all this into your lives." Her voice broke. "Daniel arrived this morning. We're flying back to Boston tomorrow. He wanted to leave today, but I told him I had to wait until you regained consciousness."

"You're flying back to Boston?" he repeated, trying to wrap his mind around the words, their meaning and his feelings about them. He had expected Anna to stay until the trial. He certainly hadn't expected to say goodbye to her under these circumstances.

"I think it's best," she said quietly, tears in her eyes. She might think it was best, but she didn't look happy about it.

Neither was he.

"Did the police find the person who planted the bomb?" he asked, changing the subject until he knew what he wanted to say and how he wanted to say it. This was important. He knew that. Anna was important, and he didn't want to make a mistake. He didn't want to have regrets in a week or a month or a year.

"Not yet. They're we're working on it," Seamus responded, pulling out his phone and sending a text to someone. "Daniel is grabbing coffee. I've let him know you're awake and that the knock on the head you received didn't damage your hard head."

"Did they review the security footage?"

"Tried. The recordings were corrupted." Seamus watched as Mac got to his feet. "That's probably not a good idea."

"When has that stopped me?" Mac grumbled, his head swimming, his vision blurring.

"You need to lie down." Anna slid an arm around his waist, trying to support him, but he was a foot taller and probably outweighed her by seventy pounds. He swayed, and she swayed with him, bumping into a bedside table and toppling a glass of ice water.

"What are you doing, man?" Daniel exclaimed as he walked into the room with a cup carry and three coffees.

"I was planning to get dressed and head home," he replied, his hand on the wall so he didn't topple over, Anna's arm still around his waist, her fingers wrapped in the teal-blue hospital gown he wore.

He wanted jeans. Flannel. Boots. His hat.

He wanted out, because hospitals were for the sick and dying, and he wasn't either of those things.

"You got thirty stitches in the back of your head. You need to stay down for a while."

"Yeah. No," he responded. "Are my clothes here somewhere?"

"Mac, this isn't a good idea," Anna murmured, still holding on.

"Neither is you going back to Boston, but that's what you're planning to do."

That was *not* what he should have said. It for sure wasn't a diplomatic way of expressing his unhappiness with the idea.

She frowned. "Okay. Fine. How about we discuss both things. After you lie down again?"

"You may as well save your breath. Once he gets an idea in that thick head of his, there's no moving him from it. If you wait out in the hall, I'll help him get dressed," Seamus said, grabbing Mac's arm and steadying him.

"I don't need help," he bit out, not wanting Anna to leave his sight. If he hadn't walked up the stairs right on her heels, if she hadn't mentioned the plant being in a different place, she'd be dead. Someone had planted the bomb. She hadn't touched it before it detonated. Someone had been watching and waiting for her return.

"I'll be out in the hall," Anna murmured, sidling away before he could catch hold of her hand.

"Be careful. Someone planted that bomb. He detonated it. That means he was on the ranch with us. It means he's someone we both know." He hated to say it. He hated that he was running through a list of likely suspects in his mind, that even in a foggy state, the betrayal was very clear to him.

"I'll make sure nothing happens to her," Daniel said, walking into the hall with her.

He wanted to call them back.

He also wanted to get dressed and get out of the hospital.

"You're stubborn as a mule, you know that?" Seamus said, opening a drawer and pulling out folded clothes.

"I need to know who did this. I need to stop him from making another move."

"You falling on your face isn't going to make either of those things happen. Sit down. I'll take the IV out."

Mac did what he asked, waiting impatiently while the catheter was removed and a paper towel used to staunch the flow of blood.

"The nurse won't be happy with me, but so be it. Go ahead and dress. I'm as anxious to get to the ranch as you are," Seamus said, grabbing a bag from the floor near the bed and holding it up. "Your house-keeper packed a few things for you. Your cell phone is in here."

"Thanks."

"I had the security footage sent to a friend of mine at a high-tech lab that specializes in video footage. He called this morning. Said he thinks he may be able to clean it up enough for us to see details."

"Good. I want to find the person responsible for this. I want him in jail. Yesterday." He nearly spat the words as he yanked on clothes, ignoring the pain in his head and the fuzziness in his mind.

Someone knocked on the door as he buttoned his shirt.

"Come in," he barked, not even trying to hide his frustration.

"Hey, Boss." Lucas Sanders walked into the room, cowboy hat in hand and a look of concern on his face. "You're looking a lot better than you did yesterday."

"Yeah. I'll feel a lot better when I know

who planted a bomb on my ranch," he responded.

"The police cordoned off the area around that cabin. They finished collecting evidence yesterday, so I brought in the bulldozer. Decided I'd better check with you before I raze what's left."

"What's left?" he asked. He hadn't thought much about the damage to his property. He'd been too busy thinking about the damage to the infrastructure of his team. He and the men and women who worked on the ranch were a family. The idea that someone in his family had tried to kill Anna and had nearly killed him in the process, infuriated and worried him.

"Just a few wooden beams and the cement foundation." Lucas shook his head. He looked drawn and tired, his normal good cheer gone. In the years they'd known each other, Mac had only ever seen him positive and energetic. He was in his mid-sixties, but in great physical shape. Most people would have guessed him to be in his early fifties. He'd aged since the explosion, his face haggard, his shoulders sloped.

"Are you okay, Lucas?"

"I'm mad as a bull with a red flag waving in front of its face. Your grandpa built that cabin for me and my wife when I came here looking for work. I'd lost my job and my house. I had nothing. He was willing to take a chance on me. Not only that, but he made it possible for me to provide a home for my wife and my two kids." He shook his head. "What happened? It was a travesty, and I can't express how sorry I am about it."

"Don't apologize for what you didn't do." Mac grabbed his coat, frowning when he saw the blood staining the back of it. "Guess this needs to be run through the wash. How about we get back to the ranch? I want to see the damage to the cabin before you raze it. We'll take pictures for insurance purposes."

"Already done," Lucas said. "I took the

liberty of contacting the insurance adjuster. He's been out. Says it'll be covered. The payout should cover the cost of building new. Although, from what I hear, Anna is leaving us. You might not need another cabin."

"Yeah. That's what I've been told."

And he still didn't like it.

But he would rather fight the battle on his own turf.

He walked into the hall, ignoring his shaky legs and his pounding head. There would be time to heal. After he made certain the person who had planted the bomb paid for it.

TWELVE

Annalise hadn't bothered returning to the ranch. She's spent the past two days and nights at the hospital, sitting beside Mac, praying that he would recover with no permanent damage. Stacey had bought her clothes, toiletries and a new cell phone. She had also sat beside Mac while Annalise showered. There was a two-inch bandage covering the deep gash in her shoulder, and she had bruises everywhere, but she was thankful to be alive.

It had been a close call.

A very close one.

She had no intention of allowing it to happen again. Not with people she cared about around.

When Daniel had arrived, he had tried to

talk her into leaving the hospital. He had suggested that she return to the ranch and pack anything she wanted to bring back to Boston.

There was nothing left to pack.

The explosion had destroyed her clothes and the few personal items she had brought from Boston. She didn't miss any of it except the photo of her and her mother. She'd kept it in a lockbox in the closet, safe from prying eyes. If she had completely followed Witness Protection rules, she would have left it behind, but she had been afraid she might never return to Boston. Or that she would return and the storage unit she had leased for a year to keep her belongings in would have been destroyed or broken into.

She had other photos of her mother, but the one she'd brought was the only one where they were both smiling, both happy, both looking as if life had treated them well. It had been taken on Mother's Day, just a few months before Annalise went to law school. Six months later, her mother had committed suicide.

When guilt left her sleepless, when she couldn't shake the feeling that she could have done more to save her mother, she would look at the photo, study her mother's smiling face, and remind herself that everything really had seemed wonderful and that there had been no hint of the deep depression her mother had fallen into.

"You're quiet," Mac said as they pulled up to the ranch's gate. They were in the back seat of Lucas's car, Seamus in the front passenger seat, his body tense as he scanned their surroundings. He had ridden to the hospital in the ambulance. Like Anna, he had stayed there, relying on a few of River's deputies to access Mac's security system and download the videos.

"Just thinking."

"About?"

"Leaving here."

"We still have to discuss that," he said,

his hand sliding over hers, their fingers twining.

"I'm not going to risk staying here. I can't risk something worse happening," she responded. "But I'll miss it."

"Like I said, we still need to discuss it. Maybe over lunch. I don't know about you, but I'm hungry."

"Only you could have an appetite with a grade three concussion," Lucas said, glancing into the rearview mirror as the gate swung open. Daniel was behind them in a rented SUV. He'd driven straight from the airport to the hospital. She wondered what he thought of the sprawling ranch with its sweeping vistas. It was a far cry from the Boston cityscape. If someone had told her six months ago that she would come to prefer it, she would have laughed, but now, her throat tightened every time she thought of leaving. Not just because of Mac. Because of the peaceful pace of life. The clean air. The feeling of belonging.

"You want to go the main house and get

something to eat? Or swing by the cabin to see the damage? If you approve, I'll start bulldozing this afternoon."

"Let's drive by. I'd like to see the damage in person."

"More likely you want to see if the police missed any clues," Seamus corrected.

"Maybe. I'd also like to make sure none of Anna's belongings can be salvaged. There is no sense bulldozing until we know for sure that nothing can be saved." He squeezed her hand, offering a reassuring smile.

Anna hadn't thought about that possibility.

She also hadn't allowed herself to toy with the idea that the lockbox might have survived the blast and the fire. She thought she had purchased a fire-resistant box, but she couldn't remember. Was it possible it had survived, and that the picture was intact?

She leaned forward as they neared the place where she had spent seven months of her life. At first, she had felt lonely and at loose ends. The frantic pace she was used to had muted the yearnings of her soul and squelched the quiet voice that echoed one of her favorite Bible verses: "Be still."

In Texas, she'd had no choice but to feel the emptiness of her life, the futility of rushing to work and home and back again. Her job was important, but friends were important too. Community was important. Reaching out instead of always dwelling in her own problems and her own worries would have been a far nobler pursuit than eating take-out Chinese food on her leather sofa, watching the latest true crime show.

She should have realized that long before she'd found herself embroiled in this mess.

She blinked back tears that had been threatening since she had walked into Mac's hospital room and seen his pale, bruised face. He had nearly died saving her. She owed him for that. If that meant leaving a place that had finally begun to feel like home, that is exactly what she planned to do.

"Well, there she is," Lucas said, pulling up in front of the blackened carcass of the old cabin. The charred remains of a few cross beams still stood defiantly. Piles of waterlogged and blackened furniture stood in the center of the ruins.

"It's okay," Mac said, brushing a tear from her cheek.

"I should be the one comforting you," she responded. "Your grandfather built this place."

"My grandfather and his father built this ranch. Most of it is still standing. I'm not going to mourn the loss of a building when lives could have been lost." He smiled, his hand still on her cheek, his eyes the silvery blue of the midnight sky.

She almost leaned toward him. Just the way she had before when their lips had touched, and she had allowed herself to believe in the revival of her childhood dreams. The family. The kids. The happy home.

But they weren't alone.

Seamus was already out of the vehicle, moving toward the cabin. Lucas was following.

"We should take a look," she said, still staring into his eyes.

"I can think of other things I'd like to do," he responded, his gaze dropping to her lips. "But you're right. This needs to be settled first. I want to know who planted the bomb, and I want him put away where he can't do any more damage." He opened his door and got out, reaching in and tugging her with him. "I still plan on having that dinner with you, Anna. If you fly back to Boston, you can expect me to come for a visit."

"Not until the trial is over," she responded, allowing herself to be led to the burnt-out shell of her former home.

"Sorry. That's not the way I operate."

"Since when are you the one calling the

shots?" she asked, smiling because she would rather be bickering with Mac than sitting beside his hospital bed. It was good to hear him talk, to see him walking and moving and acting as if nothing had happened.

"Since you decided to return to Boston without consulting me." He stepped into charred remains of the cabin, frowning as he kicked the remnants of a lamp aside. "What a mess. Did you have jewelry here? Anything of value that might have survived?"

"The only thing of value I had was a picture of me and my mom. It was in lockbox on the top shelf in the closet." She walked to the area where her room had been. The bed frame was partially standing, the mattress a pile of blackened stuffing fabric. A few burned books lay near the wrecked nightstand. The fire had burned hot, and it had burned for a while.

"A couple of the ranch hands cleared out some of the furniture and clothes. It was starting to stink, and the area was pretty ripe. They tossed it all in the burn pile. I doubt they'd have tossed a lockbox in, but you never know. I'll ask around," Lucas said, walking to the space where the closet had been. A pile of clothes lay there, as rank and horrible smelling as he had said. "They need to come back and get the rest of this. Unless you want to go through it?"

"No, but if they see the lockbox, I'd like to have it back."

"Tell you what," Lucas said. "We'll go through everything before I raze it. Shouldn't take too long. If I see the box, I'll bring it to you."

"I appreciate that."

"It's the least I can do after what happened here." He shook his head. "I must have been off my game, letting someone onto the ranch who would do something like that."

"You let someone on the ranch?" Mac asked, his voice sharp.

"Not knowingly, but how else would a

bomb have been planted? We're a family. No one would do this to family." He kicked the blackened mess of clothes and shook his head. "Come on. Let's go to the house and get some food in you before you keel over."

"I'm not going to keel over, but I would like to see the security footage that was downloaded. I want to know how it got corrupted."

"Wouldn't we all?" Seamus asked, leading the way back to the car.

Anna walked more slowly across the cement slab and the layers of burned furniture, clothes and books. She had lost everything. For the second time.

"You okay?" Mac asked.

"I don't know," she responded.

"Anything I can do to make it better?"

"Just keep being you."

He nodded, slipping an arm around her waist, his fingers curving in her belt loop. He didn't speak. She didn't need him to. She just needed to feel like she wasn't alone.

* * *

They scoured the security footage for three hours, fast-forwarding through grainy images that seemed to have been shot through a hazy lens. Mac could make out shadowy movement but no details. Head pounding, shoulders aching from being hunched over for too long, he pushed away from the table and stood.

"Did someone put plastic wrap over the security camera?" he asked, running a hand over the back of his head and prodding the swollen cut that had been stitched closed. It hurt a lot, but hurting beat being dead. He could have died. Anna could have. Seamus and River could have lost their lives. He was grateful that the only permanent damage had been done to the cabin.

"We checked for interference. We didn't find anything," Lucas said, grabbing a bowl of chips from the desk and shoving the bowl in his direction. "Eat before you fall over."

"I'm not hungry for food. I'm hungry for answers."

"That concussion is making you philosophical, Mac," Seamus said, clicking on new footage and watching it. "It's clear the day the bomb exploded. Take a look."

He rewound and played the clip again.

"One more time," Daniel said, moving closer to watch. "The plant is near the door. From what I was told, it was usually behind the cabin."

"So, the camera is clear the day of the explosion, but not the day prior," Mac murmured, something nagging at the back of his sluggish brain. "Did we watch all the footage?" he finally asked, certain they were missing something.

"Everything we have," Seamus responded. "Like I said, I've sent it to a friend who may be able to pull some images off it."

"Not if there was something blocking the lens," Daniel said. "And I agree with Mac. That's what it looks like. Someone covered the lens with a couple of layers of plastic wrap. It wouldn't be noticeable unless you looked closely, and it could be removed easily."

"You know what I'm thinking?" Seamus said, his brain apparently functioning at a faster pace than Mac's. "Fingerprints. If someone messed with the cameras, he may have left prints on the lens or on the camera."

"Good thought. I'll call the sheriff's office and ask if the cameras were dusted for prints." Daniel dialed the number and stepped out of the room.

Mac listened to the muted sound of his voice, his mind still moving toward the thing that was bothering him. They'd watched a lot of security footage. All of it from the camera installed on a tree across from the cabins. "Did anyone check the camera in the rear?" he asked, rubbing at the aching spot on the back of his head. A bandage covered the stitches, but he could feel the swollen flesh beneath it.

"I didn't realize there was a camera in the rear," Seamus responded. "But Lucas downloaded everything. You sent it all, right?"

"I sent footage from both cameras. It's in there. Probably just hard to see because of the interference. At least, it *was* there. The file was sent to the police first. Maybe I missed a section of footage when I sent it to Seamus. I'll check and let you know if I did."

"That would be good. The camera on that back fence is pointed toward the cabins rather than the cattle pen like it used to be. I switched it when Anna moved in." He hadn't believed anyone would try to get to her while she was on ranch property, but he had wanted to make certain he had a record of everything that happened near her cabin.

He should have had someone manning the security monitor. He had never felt it was necessary. He had installed the cameras on the off chance a guest was injured, had a personal belonging stolen or filed suit against the ranch. He hadn't intended the system to be monitored twenty-four hours a day.

"I want to know who did this," Mac said, the constant throbbing pain in his head a grim reminder of how close he had come to dying. His gaze shifted to Anna. She'd taken a seat on a high-backed chair against the wall. Her head was tilted back, her eyes closed.

"Looks like she's worn out," Seamus commented. "Guess you can't stay awake for forty-eight hours and not eventually give in to sleep."

"I'm not asleep," she murmured, opening her eyes and frowning. "I'm just resting my eyes."

"Maybe you should rest them in your bed," Daniel said, stepping back into the room. "We have an early flight out in the morning. We'll need to leave before dawn."

"It's three in the afternoon," she responded, barely managing to stifle a yawn.

"He's right. You should rest," Mac said. He didn't want her to leave. He wanted her to stay close so he could keep an eye on her, but there was more manpower in Boston and more of a chance that she would be safe.

That was paramount.

It was all that mattered.

"I'm not the one with thirty stitches in my head," she said with a smile that didn't hide the sadness in her eyes.

"Tell you what," he responded, pulling her to her feet. "I'll rest if you do."

"What's the catch?" she asked, allowing herself to be led from the room.

"No catch. I figure if we nap now, we can have dinner later."

"So you don't have to fly to Boston to make good on the deal?"

"So I can spend time with you before you leave. Dinner in Boston is still in the books."

"Is it?" she asked.

"Do you want it to be?" They'd reached

the guest room and stopped at the door, just a foot between them and a world of possibilities between them.

"You live in Texas. I live in Boston."

"And?"

"Long-distance relationships seldom work."

"They do if both people want them to," he responded, the pounding behind his eyes and the deadweight of fatigue on his shoulders frustrating him almost as much as the conversation suddenly was.

"Who knows how we'll feel in a week or a month or a year?" she said, the sadness in her eyes and her voice making him think she had given up before they had even tried.

"Why do we need to know? Why can't we have dinner together tonight and then in Boston? Have lunch one day in between? Call each other on the phone? Keep up until we can be together again? It's not like we can't afford to travel. It isn't like we can't make the time if we want to."

"I don't want to be hurt again. I don't want to put my trust in someone, give all my love to someone, plan a future with someone and have it all blow up in my face," she replied, and he was too tired to argue. He wasn't sure he could. How did you fight the past? How did you slay the dragons that lived in someone's heart?

"I'd hoped that you would know that I would never hurt you. I would never betray you. I certainly wouldn't walk away from you if you needed me. We're friends, Anna. You called us buddies, but I think we could have been more to each other. I think we could have been closer than just two people who like to spend time together. If you'd been willing to give it a chance." He opened the door, kissed her gently on the forehead and stepped away.

Now wasn't the time to fight this battle.

Maybe there wouldn't ever be a time for it.

Right now, he needed to get back to the office and back to the computer. There was security footage missing from the file he'd been sent. He needed to track it down. Maybe somewhere in the thousands of hours of recordings, he would find the answers they needed to stop the bomber before he could strike again.

"Mac," Anna said, touching his hand, her finger skimming lightly over his wrist. He wanted to twine his fingers through hers, pull her into his arms, and tell her that he understood.

But he didn't understand.

Not really.

He had been hurt. He had been betrayed. He was still willing to take a chance with his heart.

"Get some rest. I'll see you before you leave in the morning," he said as gently as he could, and then he walked back down the hall and left her standing alone in front of her room.

THIRTEEN

Annalise couldn't sleep.

She'd been lying in bed for hours, staring at the ceiling, calling herself a coward for not going after Mac. She had wanted to. Everything inside her had screamed that letting him walk away would be a mistake.

Like a fool, she had done it anyway.

She had been hiding in her room ever since, watching the light drift across the wall as day turned to evening and dusk turned to night. A couple hours ago, someone had knocked on the door to ask if she wanted dinner. She had pretended to be asleep. She hadn't wanted to face anyone with red eyes and a blotchy face.

Because, of course, she had been crying. Why wouldn't she be?

She had let a man she cared about—a man who had risked his life to save hers, a man who might very well be the answer to all the prayers she had prayed when she had been young enough to think she would fall madly in love, get married and grow old with a person who cherished her— walk out of her life because she had been too much of a coward to risk her heart.

"Idiot," she muttered, climbing out of bed and pacing to the window. "If you regret what you did, change it. There's still time. You're not leaving for a few hours."

The pep talk buoyed her confidence, and she walked to the door, listening to the silence of the house as she opened it. There had been a hushed murmur of voices all day, people entering the house and leaving it. Now the place seemed empty, her footsteps echoing on the hardwood floor as she walked to Mac's office. Like the main room, it was empty, the computer on.

"They're out at the cabin with the sheriff, dusting the cameras for prints," Lucas said, his voice so surprising, she jumped.

She swung to face him, smiling shakily as he walked into the room. "You scared a few years off my life."

"Sorry about that. I was heading out with them when one of the ranch hands called. He found that lockbox of yours in the burn pile and pulled it out. He's got it at the bunkhouse. I wanted to let you know." He smiled, his hands shoved deep in his pockets, his cowboy hat pulled low over his eyes.

"Really? That's fantastic."

"I knew you'd think so. I'm heading that way now, if you want to ride along. The others left a few minutes ago, so we should be able to catch up to them. We'll head to the bunkhouse first, and you can grab the box."

"That would be great," she said, running to the closet and grabbing the coat Stacey had purchased for her. "I'll grab my phone, too."

"You probably won't need it. We're not leaving the ranch," he said, offering a quick smile and glancing at his watch. "It's getting late. My wife is expecting me home soon. I need to hurry."

"I don't want to hold you up," she said, suddenly uneasy and not sure why. This was Lucas—a man Mac trusted to run his property, someone who had always been kind and willing to help. She had no reason for the gut-twisting anxiety she was suddenly feeling, but she couldn't ignore it. "Why don't you go on without me? My car didn't survive the bombing, but I'm sure I can call Stacey and catch a ride with her."

"No. Grab your phone. I'll wait." His smile had disappeared. She couldn't see his eyes beneath the rim of his hat, but she didn't think he was happy.

Something was wrong.

Really wrong.

Lucas was always smiling, always jovial, always happy.

Now he was moving toward her, his body tense, his hands fisted.

"Really, Lucas. It's fine. Go home to your wife. I'll just..."

He grabbed her arm, yanking her forward so quickly, she didn't have time to react. "I'm not going to have a wife if we don't get out of here," he muttered, dragging her toward the French doors rather than the front door. She didn't want to know the reason for that. She didn't want to think the dark thought that was rushing through her mind, either, but it was there. Lucas had access to Mac's office. He had access to the security cameras. He could have easily accessed her cabin. He had lived in it.

Was he the leak?

The bomber?

The man who had been hunting her in the woods?

The voice she had recognized when she was in the shed?

"I'm sure she's not going to leave you

because you're running late," she said, tugging away and rushing toward Mac's office. She planned to dart inside, lock the door and stay there until Mac and Seamus returned, but Lucas grabbed her from behind, his arms wrapping her in a bear hug that nearly crushed the air from her lungs.

"I don't want to do this, Anna. I hope you know that. I like you. You're a nice lady, and I would never hurt you if I didn't have to." He whispered the words, his voice harsh and panicky. A voice she recognized from the woods. One she should have recognized before now.

She tried to elbow him, but his arms were locked around hers, holding them to her sides. She wanted to kick backward and connect with his shin or his knee, but he had her off balance, her weight leaning into his, her feet sliding across the floor as dragged her to the French door and outside onto the patio. His car was parked there, edged up near an old pine tree a hundred yards away.

A hundred yards to free herself.

A hundred yards before she was tossed into his vehicle and driven to wherever he planned to dump her body.

Please, God, she prayed. *Give me the strength to escape. Please.*

"Lucas," she panted, trying to push his arms away, fighting with everything she had and still not able to budge him. "You don't have to do this."

"If I don't, they're going to kill my wife."

"Not if they go to jail," she argued, digging her heels into the ground, trying to slow their progress. Hadn't anyone realized that Lucas had disappeared? Wasn't anyone wondering why he wasn't around?

Probably not.

He was like the snake in the garden, spouting beautiful words to hide the darkness in his heart.

"Go to jail? Do you know how many people have died trying to put Moreno there?"

"What do you have to do with him? How do you even know him?"

"I don't. I know his associates. They loan money, and they like to be paid back on time. With interest," he growled.

"So pay them back. If you don't have the money, I'll lend it to you."

"It's not that easy. Not anymore. Moreno heard you were hiding near Abilene. Someone in the Justice Department is in his pocket. The people I owe money? They want the reward he's offering to…take care of his problem. They've been showing your picture to everyone who owes them. I said I'd seen you. I thought that would be enough. It wasn't." They'd reached the car. He had to loosen his grip to open the door.

She slammed her elbow into his gut, and ran, screaming loudly, all the terror she'd been feeling since the night of the shooting bubbling out. She rounded the corner of the house, knowing he was right behind her. She could hear his panting breath and pounding feet.

She was nearly to the front yard, still screaming when he tackled her, knocking her off her feet and sending her skidding across the grass. Breath knocked from her lungs, she tried to scramble up again.

He slammed her back down, yanked a gun from beneath his coat. "I didn't want this. I didn't want any of it," he said.

"Then, change it," she replied.

"Too late." He slammed the butt of the gun against her temple. She saw stars, felt herself drifting into unconsciousness. She fought it, refusing to give in as he dragged her to the car and tossed her into the back seat.

She lay where she landed, limp. Still. Hoping he wouldn't shoot her there. If he drove to another location, she might have a chance to escape.

He slammed the door and jumped into the driver's seat, muttering under his breath as he started the engine and pulled away. Slowly. No rush. No hurry. Pretending, as he always had, that he was doing nothing wrong.

* * *

Something was bothering him.

Still.

Mac had been rolling thoughts around in his head, trying to make sense of his unease. It had something to do with the camera on the fence behind the cabins.

He stared at it as the sheriff's deputies dusted for prints, his mind clicking along at a sluggish pace that left him frustrated. He wanted to go back to the house and check on Anna. She hadn't responded to his knocks at her door. She hadn't answered when Stacey had asked her if she wanted to eat. She was sound asleep, or she was hiding. Either way, he wanted to make sure she was okay.

He hadn't meant to pressure her.

He wanted a relationship. One that went far beyond buddy status, but he would be content to be friends. He had realized that as he'd watched looped security footage of the explosion and its aftermath. Every time the plant exploded, his heart raced.

Every time, he found himself wanting to do even more to protect Anna.

He had watched as she'd crawled out from under him. Watched as she'd dragged him away from the shooting flames. He'd had no memory of any of it, but now he knew what she had done. The way she had removed her coat to stop his bleeding and followed his gurney to the ambulance as her arm dripped blood.

She was the kind of person he wanted in his life.

The kind of person he didn't want to lose.

If keeping her around meant staying in the friendship zone, that was what he would do.

"What's bugging you?" Seamus asked, his question right to the point. No doubt at all that something was bothering Mac. They knew each other too well for that.

"I don't know. Something about the camera, but I can't figure out what."

"That one in particular?" he asked, gesturing to the fence and the sheriff's deputies.

"Yes."

"Maybe it's something to do with the fact that your foreman didn't download the security footage?" he said.

"Lucas? He said he did."

"He was mistaken, or he lied. I checked with the sheriff's office. Had them send the file they received. It was the same as the one we have here."

"That doesn't make sense. He would have..." Mac stopped, everything suddenly clicking into place, his mind and his thoughts sharply focused. "Where is he?"

"Lucas? He left ten minutes ago. Said he was heading home. Why?"

"He didn't know I'd turned the camera. I've always had it facing the pasture. I turned it before Anna arrived, but I didn't tell anyone, because no one was supposed to know she was in Witness Protection or that I wanted to keep a careful eye on her."

"If he thought the camera was turned toward the pasture, why would he download footage from it?" Seamus frowned. "He didn't download the footage, because he thought the camera was turned away from the cabins. So, he lied. Why?"

"Because, he didn't cover the camera lens like he did the one on the tree, and he was trying to buy time so he could access the footage himself and delete it," Mac responded grimly.

"He set the bomb, then." It wasn't a question. They both knew the truth.

"Let's go. If he headed back to the house, he already has a ten-minute head start on us." He sprinted to the road, adrenaline shooting through him and stealing away the pain and fatigue.

Lucas, a man he had known and trusted for nearly twenty years, had placed the bomb. He was the traitor, and Anna was alone at the house, completely unaware that he couldn't be trusted.

"What's going on?" Daniel rolled up beside him in his SUV, shoving open the door so Mac could scramble in. Seamus shoved him into the console and climbed in beside him.

"It's Lucas. He's the one who's been after Anna. I don't know why I didn't realize it before," he growled, slamming his hand onto the dashboard. "He had access to everything. He has free run of the ranch, including my office. He could have easily planted the tracking device."

"Think about what you're saying," Daniel responded. "He could have killed her a dozen times over. No one suspected him. He had easy access to her. Maybe—"

"He wouldn't kill her here. He wanted it to look like an accident. Or like she walked into the wilderness and disappeared. Think about *that*. You know Moreno's MO better than I do, but all a person has to do is read a few newspaper articles and it's clear that people who cross him aren't usually found. They're gone. Dropped off the face of the earth so there's no way to connect him to their deaths. That's how he has stayed out of prison for so long."

"Right," Daniel muttered. "That's his MO. Make them disappear. Or they commit suicide. Every once in a while, there's an accident, but people who cross him aren't usually murdered. Until the courthouse shooting. His big mistake."

"It's only a mistake if Anna survives to testify against him," Mac said, leaning forward as they approached the house. It looked normal. Almost. He could see scuff marks in the rocky path near the side of the house and tire tracks in the grass.

"He's been here, and he's gone," he said, knowing without going inside that Anna was gone, too.

"We need to check on Anna," Daniel said.

"He had her. Look at the marks in the grass and on the path. There was a struggle, and he drove off."

"Has he made it to the gate yet?" Seamus asked. "Is there any way to send deputies to cut him off before he hits the road?"

"I can lock down the gate and freeze the

code so it can't be opened. If he hasn't left. Wait here." Mac jumped out and ran into the house, punching numbers into the security panel on the wall and locking down the gate.

When he returned to the SUV, Seamus was on the phone, calling in for a roadblock. Mac scrambled into the back seat, praying that Lucas was still inside the gate as Daniel accelerated down the driveway.

They were halfway to the gate when he saw the car, parked in front of the gate, the driver's door open. A backdoor was open, too. The SUV screeched to a halt behind the vehicle, and Mac jumped out.

"They can't have gone far," Seamus said, glancing inside the car. "No blood on the seats. No sign that anyone was injured."

"There are plenty of injuries that don't bleed," Mac responded grimly, scanning the fields beside the driveway.

He saw nothing. Just fences. Fields. Trees.

"We need to split up," he said. "Look for tracks. There is no way they walked through the wet field without leaving some. If you find something, holler. We'll follow on foot. If Anna is conscious, she's fighting to slow him down."

If.

He hated saying that.

He hated knowing that she could be unconscious, helpless, injured.

Worse.

Please, God, help us find her, he prayed as he crouched near the car and looked for the first set of prints.

FOURTEEN

Anna couldn't breathe.

She couldn't move.

She could barely think.

But she *could* hear voices.

She knew help was close.

If she could just push Lucas's huge body away, get his hand off her mouth, she could scream. She hadn't escaped the car to die in a field. She could do this. She had no choice.

"Don't even think about moving," he growled in her ear, pressing the gun to her temple. "I will kill you here, if I have to."

She wanted to ask what difference it made where she died, but his hand was so tight against her lips, she thought she'd have bruises. Not that it would matter if she was dead.

Grass rustled a few yards away. She wanted to turn her head, but it was pressed into the ground, her body held down by his heavy weight.

Whoever it was moved closer.

She could see a figure silhouetted against the sky, and she wanted to call out a warning.

Lucas raised the gun.

She couldn't let this happen. Not again. She wouldn't.

She bucked as hard as she could, throwing him sideways as the gun exploded. It flew from his hands, landing in thick grass. Her ears rang, but she was nearly free. She pushed him away, kicking and punching as she tried to break his hold.

He grabbed her neck, tossing her to the ground, strangling her, and she was helpless to stop him, her body flopping like a rag doll's as she tried to knock him away.

He growled, slamming her deeper into

the ground, his knee pressed into her abdomen to keep her still. And she was fading away, losing her grip on the world.

Then, she was breathing. Gasping. Coughing. Choking as air filled her lungs.

Someone was holding her shoulders.

Gently, though. Hands cupping her back as she tried to catch her breath. "Anna, are you okay?" Mac asked, smoothing hair from her face and looking into her eyes.

"Yes. Lucas..."

"Seamus has him. There are deputies on the way. He's going to jail. And he'll be there for a long time," he said grimly.

"He said they were going to kill his wife. Someone needs to go make sure she's okay."

"Who is going to kill his wife?" Daniel asked, crouching next to her, his gaze filled with concern.

"He didn't give me names. He just said he owed people money, and that they know Moreno. They want the money he's offering for my...death."

"And if Lucas killed you, it would pay off his debt?"

"I'm assuming so. He didn't go into a lot of details, and I didn't have a lot of time to ask questions. He did say that Moreno got information about me being near Abilene, Texas, from someone in the Justice Department."

"I know," Daniel said. "We've suspected a leak, and we've been tracking two people we thought might have been responsible. One of them was taken into custody earlier today. We have phone records linking him to one of Moreno's associates."

"That would have been good to know before Lucas tried to choke the life out of her," Mac grumbled, taking off his jacket and wrapping her in it.

"I would have told you, but we were still sifting through information, trying to get a handle on who planted that bomb."

"You're not going to say you suspected me, I hope." Mac stood and helped Anna to her feet.

"As you've said before, everyone is a suspect until he isn't."

"Everything okay over here?" Seamus asked, striding toward them through the long grass.

"Is it?" Mac asked Anna, touching her cheek, his fingers skimming the curve of her jaw and the column of her neck. "You're going to have bruises."

"You're going to have a scar," she replied, dizzy with relief, but sad for what Mac had lost. One of his closest and most trusted friends had betrayed him. That would hurt for a long time.

"There are worse things," he said, leading her through the grass and onto the road. There were two marked police cars there. One inside the gate. One outside. She knew Lucas was in one car, cuffed and waiting to be driven away.

"I need to go to the house to unlock the gate," Mac called to a uniformed deputy who stood near one of the cars.

"No problem. We're in no hurry. We've

got all night to book this guy." He smiled. "We'll need to get statements, too. Sheriff Williams said you can come in tomorrow to give them."

"We will," Mac said, his arm slipping around Anna's waist. She leaned into his side, enjoying the warmth of his touch and the comfort it brought.

"I have a car, you know," Daniel called.

"You want to ride?" Mac asked Anna.

"You know, I think I'd rather walk. It gives us more time to talk."

"About?"

"Dinner in Boston."

"And lunch?"

"That, too."

"FaceTime calls?"

"And lots of visits," she said, because it felt right. He felt right.

"Absolutely." He stopped, turning so they were face-to-face. "I love you, Anna. I want to say that before you leave tomorrow. As a friend. As a buddy. As something more than both those things."

"I love you, too. As a friend and a buddy and more," she responded, looking into his eyes and knowing that she could look for the rest of her life and it would never be enough.

He smiled, kissing her gently, sweetly. All the moments they'd shared leading to this perfect one.

The police cruiser was behind them, Daniel and Seamus talking to the deputy. She was still in danger. Until the trial, she knew she would never be completely safe, but standing with Mac, moonlight streaming between gray clouds, she had the soul-deep feeling that everything was going to be okay.

"Ready?" he asked, pulling back and taking her hand again.

"To go to the house?"

"For whatever the future brings."

"If I'm with you? Absolutely," she responded.

"You know what? That's exactly how I feel." He kissed her knuckles, squeezed her hand, and they walked down the road together. Side by side. Friends. Buddies. More. Ready to face the future. Together.

EPILOGUE

The sun shone brightly on golden fields of corn as Annalise drove the last few miles to Sweet Valley Dude Ranch. Winter had given way to spring. Spring to summer. She had the windows open, balmy air blowing in as she sang along with her favorite worship music. The trial had ended four days ago, the long legal process pushing the date out so many times, she had begun to think it would never happen.

And then it had.

Mac had been there, holding her hand as she waited to testify, reassuring her that she was under close guard and that it would be over soon. He had stayed in an adjoining room in a hotel near the courthouse where Anna had been under constant guard for so many months, she had begun to feel like a prisoner.

Federal police had raided the office of the loan sharks who had threatened Lucas's wife. They'd arrested the men who Lucas said had been with him when he had hunted her through the forest. They'd neutralized every threat they could, and they had believed she was safe, but they hadn't been willing to take any chances. Reginald Boeing had given the police information that had led to Archie's arrest, and federal and local police had done everything necessary to keep Annalise safe until the trial.

For Mac's sake, she had agreed to their rules. She'd stayed close to her armed guards. She had done most of her work remotely. She had lived her life in a gilded cage, and now, she was finally free. Archie had been tried and convicted. He and Boeing would spend the rest of their lives in jail.

Annalise was safe, and she couldn't stop smiling as she pulled up to the ranch gates.

Home, the wind seemed to whisper as they swung open.

Finally.

And if she had her way, forever.

She had put in for a transfer, asking to work in the Dallas field office. It was a three-hour drive, but much closer than Boston. If the FBI refused her request— and it didn't look like that would happen— she already had offers from two law firms.

She could rent a small apartment in Dallas and buy a house in Briarwood. She had grown to love the small town and the people in it. She never would have expected it, but God had known. He had been working His plan for her life during the hardest times.

And, now, He was bringing her home.

She parked in front of the house, knowing that Mac was probably out in the pasture. It was calving season, and things were hectic. He had hired a new foreman, and he had told her that things were going well, but she worried about him. About the heartache of losing someone he had been so close to.

She opened the front door, stepping into the great room and stopping short when she saw Mac standing near the fireplace.

"Mac! I thought you'd be out working."

"And miss greeting you when you arrived? Not a chance." He pulled her into his arms and into a kiss that made her toes curl in her stiletto heels.

"Wow," she murmured against his lips.

"I was thinking the same," he said, smiling into her eyes. "I've missed you."

"You left Boston three days ago," she reminded him.

"Like I said, I've missed you."

She laughed, leaning back so she could study his face. "I love you. I'm thrilled to see you, but it's calving season. You need to do your thing. I'll do mine."

"Which would be?"

"I'm going to help Stacey in the kitchen. I've missed her."

"And she's missed you, but before we both act responsibly, I have something for you." He lifted a wrapped package from the mantel and handed it to her.

"What is it?" she asked, her hands shaking. It had been years since she had been given a present, and she felt teary-eyed from the sweetness of the surprise.

"You'll know once you open it," he responded, making her laugh as she carefully pulled back the paper and revealed a mahogany frame with a photo inside. At first, what she was seeing didn't register. Two women smiling into each other's eyes. One of them holding a bouquet of flowers.

Mother's Day flowers.

Her mom. Annalise.

It was the photo she'd thought lost in the fire.

"Mac," she said.

Nothing else, because she couldn't get the words out past the lump in her throat.

"I searched through the rubble until I found the box. The photo was a little water-damaged, but I was able to have it restored."

"I can't believe you did this for me." She threw her arms around him, hugging him tight, the framed photo between them. "Thank you."

"I would do anything for you. I hope you know that."

"And I would do anything for you," she responded.

"Even put the photo here?" he asked, taking it from her hands and setting on the mantel next to photos of his grandparents, of him, of his parents and cousins and siblings.

"If that's where you want it," she responded.

"What I want is for your mother to be family. Not just yours. Mine, too. And I want us both to wake up every morning and see the picture of her mixed with pictures of all the other people we love and have loved."

"That's a sweet, thought, Mac, but it's going to be hard to see the picture every day when I'm in Dallas."

"You got the transfer?" he asked, his eyes bright with enthusiasm and joy.

"Not yet. But I think I will, and even if I don't, I'm moving here to Texas. Being back in Boston convinced me that I'm not an indoor kind of gal."

"What kind of gal are you, then?" he asked with smile.

"The kind that wants to be close to you," she responded.

"I'm glad to hear that, because I love you, Anna. I want to spend the rest of my life with you." He pulled a ring from the pocket of his jeans. No fancy jeweler's box. No fanfare. "Will you marry me?"

"Yes," she said, her voice trembling, her heart full.

He slipped the ring on her finger, the old mine cut diamond sparkling as he lifted her hand and kissed her knuckles. "I love you. For today. For tomorrow. For always."

"I love you, too. For as many days as the sun shines and as many nights as the moon glows." She stepped into his arms, kissing him with passion and joy and love. When they finally broke apart, she was breathless, frazzled and happier than she could ever remember being.

"Ready?" he said, taking her hand and leading her outside.

"For what?" she asked.

"To spend the rest of our lives together."

"Absolutely," she responded, walking with him toward the pastures, the sun bright overhead, the fields lush with life, her heart filled to overflowing.

With gratitude.

With thanksgiving.

With love.

* * * * *

*If you enjoyed this story,
be sure to pick up these
other exciting books
by Shirlee McCoy:*

Night Stalker
Gone
Dangerous Sanctuary
Lone Witness
Falsely Accused

*Available now from
Love Inspired Suspense!*

Find more great reads at
www.LoveInspired.com

Dear Reader,

Until recently, I hadn't realized what a difficult taskmaster I was. Not toward others, but toward myself. How critical of my achievements and how disappointed in my failures I tended to be. As I have extended grace to those who have hurt me, friends have reminded me that I am worthy of grace too. We are all fallible, prone to mistakes, often dogmatic in our positions and thoughtless in our actions. But love erases that. *His* love. *His* grace. *His* mercy. He demands nothing of us except that we offer the same as we move through this world. Not just to others, but to ourselves. When you look in the mirror today, I pray that you will see yourself as He does: loved, forgiven and redeemed. Wherever you are in life, whatever your heartache and pain, please know that you matter to Him and to me.

I love to hear from readers. You can